This book is dedicated to Philippa, Ruth and Patrick.
And Dan, our other *dramatis persona.*

CONTENTS

Sky Light

We sang hymns and drank beer straight from the bottle the day the harmonium arrived. Its dead weight made us sweat and graze our knuckles on the wall of the stair-well as we carried it up the four flights of stairs to her tenement flat.

But Sheila rewards us with the beer.

"Why a harmonium?"

"I love them." she says.

"...but why?"

"I love the sound. It's beautiful."

And later she picks out some hymns. *To be a pilgrim* and *The day Thou gavest Lord is ended.* Then she tells us that the devil has all the best tunes and plays a mazurka, but ends with *Abide with Me* to lead us in our singing. Our noise fills the room, sharp edged against the reedy softness of the harmonium notes. The singing and the tune float out of the skylight of her flat into the night. For the rest of the evening we drink her beer until we fall asleep where we are. When we awake, Sheila has gone to work her weekend shift, so we spend the morning hanging around in her flat. We play her albums, make breakfast and do a bit of tidying up. She lives on her own, has two young children to bring up and works hard. We all like to help.

Before we leave, I open the skylight to let in some air. I stand with my head out of the window and look out across the roofs, open spaces then the treetops to where the distant hills are blue and green in the clear sky. I turn around from the opening when the noise of my friends fooling around comes from the kitchen. Sheila has pinned a note to the inside of the door to remind us to lock-up as we leave. She's been burgled before and she's wary. We tell her she should move, but she asks, "Where to?"

I look around Sheila's small living room. There is a potted plant on the ledge above her fire place, with a crimson flower floating like a planet in the tightness of her flat. Next to it is a bowl of fruit; bright green apples catching the sun from the skylight.

Where I grew up there was an orchard at the end of town. My mate at school, Gregor, told me about it. He said it was just beyond the last houses, where the farms began to spread out. He said we could get into it over the fence. He told me that the trees, particularly the apple trees, had fruit bigger than he'd ever seen.

"Where ?"

"I'll show you." he said.

"When."

"Sometime...I've been loads of times. "

"On your own?"

"Mostly."

He told me we should go there and I said yes and he said no more for several days. But he didn't forget and he pulled me into his plans to go back to the orchard when the apples were ripe. He said that we would need to bunk-off school because there would be too many people around on a weekend.

I was already worried about it, so I convinced him we should do it after school and we settled for that. As we sat in his bedroom, he told me too of an empty house on his estate. It had been boarded up by the Council but he said he knew a way in.

He lived in a flat in a new high-rise block. He shared a bedroom with a brother who was not there very often. We sat and stared out of his window at the other tower blocks and the streets below, and thought of how we could get to the orchard. As he talked I looked around his room. Apart from the two beds there was only a single wardrobe, the door of which was hanging off. There was a poster of a sports car on the wall. The room felt grey and empty. Through the window I watched the people cross the open spaces below us. Some boys from our school were kicking a football around against the lock-up garage doors. Through the window, from down below, I heard the boys shouting football songs as they played. Then they started to chant, "You're going to get your fucking head kicked in."

When I arrive the next day, Sheila is playing her harmonium. I hear it from the flight of stairs below her front door. It is a soft, breathless sound. As I reach her front door I can hear the sound of her feet moving the pedals to operate the bellows. A gentle, rhythmic rocking which cuts through the tempo of the tune. I wait until she has finished before I ring the bell.

"Don't stop." I say as I go into her room.

"I've been at it for ages."

"You're good."

"I'm crap."

I make us coffee and we talk. She tells me about Fiona, one of our friends. Fiona has two teenage children, who she doesn't hear from anymore. She gets to hear about them from people around the city, including Sheila. They turn up in a squat or in a friend's house somewhere; they get into relationships and leave them. "Of course she worries. I hear about them from time to time," Sheila says as she shows me a few chords on the harmonium. "I shouldn't tell her about them. It's supposed to be confidential, but what do you do? They're her kids."

We sit next to each other as she plays the right-hand melody and I play my new chords on the left hand. She moves the stops in and out to change the volume and the tone.

"You're a natural," she says.

"Yeah. Sure."

"We'll get you onto the right hand soon."

"I can't do two things at once."

She thinks that Fiona's girls are on hard drugs; she wouldn't be surprised if they were. Fiona just wants to know where they are, but she's got to stay sane herself, and she can't worry about them all the time. "That's why I do some of the worrying for her," says Sheila.

As I leave, she begins to play another tune, and its melody follows me down the flights of stairs, but I also imagine it drifting upwards through the skylight. I look up at her window before I walk off down the street.

As I approached Gregor's block of flats, I looked up towards his window on the seventh floor. Gregor had been grounded. He had been to the boarded-up house again to try to get in. The police had caught him trying to kick open the door along with his brother and took them to the station to be cautioned.

Their mother had been down to collect them. When she opened the door for me, she looked at me as if she wanted to hit me. I was scared of her. Gregor said she was OK though.

"He's in his room," she said.

"Thanks."

"He can't go out."

"No," I said.

"He's a little shit."

In Gregor's room he told me about the boarded-up house and the things he was going to do in there. I did not remind him about the trip to the orchard. He told me instead about smoking and drinking bottles of cider. He thought that his friend sniffed glue and that his brother's friend might be taking drugs. I asked if he had ever taken drugs, but he said that he'd not.

As he talked, I ended up staring out of the window again. Not long after that I left. I shouted goodbye to his mother but she didn't reply. She was watching the television.

Out on the concrete square between the towers, I looked back up at his window. He was still sitting there and I waved. He waved back. I felt sorry for him. He was so distant, framed in the window high up in the tower block. He looked down at the square below where I was standing and where the boys were playing football.

They were shouting and swearing at each other as usual. Some were wearing proper football kit. My mother couldn't afford it, so I just did without. I wasn't really bothered. As the boys played, one of them kicked the ball so hard it bounced against the garage doors and rebounded towards where I was walking. I was hoping that they would not notice me, but the ball rolled straight towards me. I stopped it with my foot, and it bobbled slightly. Then it kept rolling slowly down the hill. I wanted to kick it back, but couldn't get properly behind it because it had not stopped moving. So I kept shuffling to try to get in a better position.

Eventually one of the boys shouted out, "Kick it back you wanker."

So I kicked it as best I could and it rolled pathetically towards them.

"You fucking Jessie", shouted one of the boys and they laughed. I walked on and just before I turned off towards my house, I looked back. The boys had carried on playing football and Gregor was still at the window. I waved again, but he must have been watching the game, as he didn't wave back.

A few of us meet up after work to get a drink and something to eat, and I phone Sheila to let her know. She says that she might come along. When I arrive in the restaurant after work, she's already there with some of our friends and my work mates. The two groups kind of blend into each other. Most of us are in similar jobs – the worrying professions she calls them - and everyone knows each other one way or other.

Sheila is sitting and laughing with a couple of her female friends, so I sit with my colleagues. I am at the end of the table because I am late, but she looks up and gives a little wave. She also imitates playing the harmonium with her hands and laughs some more. Her friend nudges her and I watch Sheila turn to her and explain what the mime was about.

The noise we make drowns out the music and the other conversations in the room. It is a dark and claustrophobic basement with a low barrel vault ceiling. It is just brick that has been painted over. My colleagues gossip about work and I join in as best I can. Two people are having an affair, it seems. I cannot picture either of them, but I go along with the conversation.

"They should know better," says Malkie.

"They must both be over forty-five."

"Sex sweeps all before it."

Then they then ask me who I fancy in the office; who would I have an affair with. The people around us have joined in the conversation, so they are egging me on to answer.

"I've never really thought about it," I say.

"Sure you have."

"What about Becky here," says Malcolm, putting his arm round one of the women. "She's good for a shag," he says and they all laugh. They laugh so loud that the rest of the table turns round to look at us. Becky lets out a short scream at Malcolm, but then laughs as well. She slaps him lightly on the arm, too.

"He says he wants to shag Becky," says Malcolm looking up towards the rest of the table and pointing at me. I just smile as they all look on. Sheila raises her eyebrows in mock surprise, and then pours herself and her friends another glass of wine. I too reach for a bottle and pour a glassful.

When I go round, Sheila is standing at her front door, grinning.

"So, you want to shag Becky," she says.

"That's not what I said."

"Sure," and she opens the door fully.

I step through, but she tells me that she is just on her way out. She has some news about Fiona's children and she is on her way to try to get in touch with them. She has an address on one of the estates at the edge of town. She has a work car to get her there. I offer to go with her.

"It might not be pretty." she says.

"I'll cope."

"Where are your kids?" I ask.

"They're at their dad's."

The car is a small, bright yellow and with the words Social Services written on it.

"Not much chance of sneaking up in this, then," I say.

We're going to look at the address we have and, Shelia tells me, officially we can't do anything as the girls are both over sixteen. Fiona just wants to make sure they're alright. She has even considered registering them as missing persons, but then they might leave the city.

"She doesn't know what to do."

"I'm not sure I would, either," I say.

The journey to the housing estate is slow. It's the start of the after-work rush and the roads are crowded, firstly with cars then, as we get out into the housing schemes, more and more buses. Here the streets are emptier. It has taken nearly an hour to travel the relatively short distance and the difference between here and the city centre is vast. I have forgotten just how these estates feel. Not since I used to visit Gregor have I really been back to places like this. We look at the long list of street names at the entrance to each part of the estate. Every road leading to another street leading to another one. They are named after people, after other towns, after long gone features. *Croft Road* or *Orchard Place*. Blocks of flats named after foreign politicians. We turn round in a bus turning circle, which is full of broken glass, and on our way back, we see the name of the street we're looking for.

"Into the valley of death." says Sheila turning in.

"What?"

"It's a poem," she says.

There are only two other cars in the parking area. In one corner are the remains of a litter bin that has been burned. We get out and head towards the block of flats. The lift does not work so we walk the seven floors to the floor we want. I am worried, but Sheila seems relaxed as she knocks on the door.

"Who is it?" The voice is feint. The woman sounds drunk.

"It's Sheila McVeigh."

"And who the fuck is Shelia McVeigh?"

"I've come to see Fiona Gibson's daughters."

"Well they're not fucking here."

We wait and Sheila speaks again. This time, after a short while, the person comes to the door, and opens it slowly and only partly. The girl inside is small and slight, skinny almost. It's one of Fiona's daughters. She is high on something. Her eyes are red and wander as if they are on bits of string. Her skin is pale and yellow.

She and Sheila talk on the doorstep for a short-while as I stand further away. Then Sheila calls me over. We go into the flat. It smells of urine and despair. The mattresses are on the floor and the sheets are filthy. There's no furniture. A small CD player lies in pieces in the corner with a few CDs scattered around the room along with mobile phones and a pile of empty pizza boxes. Fiona's daughter sits on the mattress with her knees drawn up to her chest and her back to the wall as Sheila asks her how she is and does she want anything. She bends down and squats in front of the girl, who does not look at her. I cannot hear what either of them is saying, so I go out of the flat.

Outside, I look over the balcony onto the ground below. I can see the car, and some lock-up garages. There is a sign, saying no ball games but a couple of kids are kicking a ball around. Beyond the houses and the tower blocks, the city centre is visible. The big Victorian and Georgian buildings massed together, crowding in towards the main square. Beyond those are the streets of tenements and houses where Sheila and I live. And Sheila's skylight that lets the harmonium notes out into the night.

Gregor's mum was Catholic; I knew that from the pictures and things on the walls.

My mother brought us up Catholic. She went to Mass every week; the rest of us tried to avoid it, but sometimes she made us go. Me and my sister had to walk with her to the big ugly church. She said that the Protestants took all of the pretty churches years ago and left us with nothing, so we had to build the new ones; ours was always empty except for a few of my mum's friends. But we sang and our thin voices rose into the roof of the draughty church. She had things up on our wall; the cross, the sacred heart, a picture of Lourdes.

Gregor's mum opened the door next time I went round and spoke without me saying anything.

"He still can't come out, you know?"

"I know."

Her front room was clean and tidy and the walls were bare, except for a picture of Christ and the sacred heart on the wall next to Gregor's bedroom door. She had a model lighthouse on the fireplace and a picture of Gregor in his school uniform. I went into his room. He was sitting on his bed.

We talked about the boarded-up house and his brother. His brother had been caught doing drugs and had to go to court. Gregor said his mum was really mad, "But mostly she cries a lot," he said.

Then I suddenly said to Gregor, for no reason that I could think of, "I'm going to go to that orchard."

"When?" he said

"Tomorrow. Before we go back to school."

"Wait for me. Until my mum lets me out."

"I can't."

And I sat on his bed and half-looked out of the window and half-listened to him. He talked of how he would come with me to the orchard when he could get out again and how we could break into the boarded-up house and drink some lager. In the Christmas holidays we would bunk off the school concerts and go into the city centre.

"We don't have to waste our time singing carols," he said. It's as if mentioning the orchard had opened his eyes again to things outside his room. "My mum gets worse at Christmas," he said. "She goes all religious and goes to church nearly everyday for a week so she'll never miss us."

The silence rushed in when he stopped talking. Soon after this I left when Gregor had told me which bus to catch to get to the orchard.

"They're the biggest apples ever." he added, almost as an afterthought.

Down on the concrete square, I looked up again at his window, but he was not there. The boys were not playing football.

Walking back to Sheila's car, I look up at the windows of the block of flats. I am not sure which one we have just been in. Sheila tells me that it is no use looking, as Fiona's daughter will be inside the flat on her mobile phone, the one she gets given to do the deals on, arranging to move to another flat. She will be telling her older sister that they have been found. That is not what they wanted. But she had also promised to get in touch with Fiona, just to let her know what has happened.

"At least I can tell her they're alive."

"You were brilliant up there," I say

"Just doing my job, sir," she says in a mock American accent.

On our way out of the estate we take a wrong turning and end up heading away from the city, out up towards the hills that ring that edge of the built-up area. The pylons begin to spread out, marching ankle deep in mud across the ploughed fields towards the horizon. The houses and blocks of flats stop abruptly as we cross the bridge over the ring road. Here there are scrappy fields with thin hedgerows where horses graze,.

"I'm lost." says Sheila.

"Long term or short term?" I ask.

She drives up the road to look for a turning place. Behind us, the tower blocks are as pale as dead trees against the evening sky. In a lane about a mile or so up the hill we come to somewhere that the landscape around me looks vaguely familiar. There is a lane, with a couple of houses at each corner. A woman is at the kitchen window in one of the houses, standing at the sink looking out onto the side road. A man is walking his dog away from us along the lane. A sprinkler is going on someone's lawn. These small collisions in our lives make me think even more that I know the place, that I even know these people, but then perhaps I have just seen so many places like this on the urban fringe, they all blend into one. But I still ask Sheila to drive further up the lane. Just in case.

"There's a farm at the end of this lane," I say.

"There always is."

"No. I've been here before.... I think."

"Long term or short term?" she asks.

We pass the man with the dog. He watches us go past as he stands in the verge out of our way. Sheila waves a *thank you* to him as we pass. He does not respond. We drive along the lane, running parallel to the edge of the city and the ring road, until eventually we arrive at a farm which has buildings on both sides of the road. In a yard, a worker is moving large cylindrical straw bales with a tractor and forklift attachment. He too watches us pass. I had forgotten about the colour and wording on the van. We go past the farm buildings and again the lane is lined with scrappy hedges.

"Stop here," I shout as we pass a gate.

I get out and Sheila stands next to me looking over the gate, up the hill away from the city.

"It might be the place," I say.

"What place?"

"Somewhere I came when I was young."

We look at the hill and follow its slope towards the horizon.

From the bus, I walked up the road away from the city and then turned down a lane, as Gregor had told me. He'd wanted to come with me and promised to take me to the boarded-up house with him if I did wait. I wanted to come on my own, though. The lane worried me. It was like nowhere that I was used to walking. What if someone saw me? What if they asked what I was doing? I did see a farm, and beyond it the fields and hedges. But I did not see an orchard.

I walked past the farmhouse and the out-buildings and on the other side of the farm a high wall ran along the road-side. There was still no orchard. I began to believe that there wasn't one, or I'd got the wrong place altogether. I walked on a bit further, but then after I passed the farm and turned a corner out of view, I stopped.

"There is no bloody orchard," I thought.

So I climbed over a gate and followed a track away from the road, down the hill towards the city's edge. And I saw a tree in the corner of the field that had low branches and a good flat top. I thought to myself that I would climb it. It looked like easy climbing, with strong branches and firm footholds. I pulled myself up onto the lower branches. For a short while I disappeared into the limbs and branches. I couldn't see anything around me, but I could see ahead of me, where the sky's light was coming through the crown. So I kept climbing. Gradually the small twigs began to thin out and then my head emerged from the top of the tree and I could see all around me. I found a good point to sit and I gazed out over the fields from my seat in the sky. I saw the farm, I saw the road I'd come along and, in the other direction, I could see the city. I could see Gregor's tower block and, just beyond that, the area where I lived. I could see everything from there.

"Let's go," I say to Sheila.

"I didn't want to stop."

"I just thought…" I start to say.

Back in the car we head towards the city. In the evening sunlight the stonework and older buildings glow deep red.

"It's a really beautiful city," I say.

"I love it."

"Do you fancy a drink...something to eat?"

"Why, who's going out?"

"No-one...just you and me I mean."

She is silent for a short moment. Then she says, "Yes...I do. That would be great. That would be really, really great." And, in the silence that follows, as we head back into the city, I imagine her words floating like music up into the evening light, caught by the gentle air.

On The Edge

The man on the television was crying.

His lined face, large and tanned, was set against a background of pale mountains. His turban was coming loose. The camera panned back to show him holding the body of a child as he explained that his own countrymen had been attacking his village with gas. His eyes flicked like those of a trapped animal between the camera and the interviewer. He wanted someone to help him understand.

I watched the footage of dead mothers and fathers lying over the bodies of their children, having tried vainly and naïvely to protect them from the invisible cloud. Then, when the camera cut back to the man, he started to cry. He moaned and then rocked backwards and forwards with grief as he explained that he had been at market in a distant town, so missing the attack. He said that he wished he was also dead then stared silently at the camera, waiting.

They called me on the radio, so I turned off the television. They told me a storm was coming and that they were concerned for me. I said I knew about the storm. I had seen the weather forecasts that they regularly emailed to me so of course I knew about the storm. I was my job to know about the storm.

"We are worried about you."

"I'm OK," I said.

"But you're on your own."

"I volunteered to be here."

"That's not the point."

"I'll survive."

"I'm sure you will." I turned to watch the gannets through the window next to the desk in my office. They are large awkward birds on land, but once they are in the water, they are powerful and so perfectly shaped. Pure white knives cutting silently into the ocean. They rarely come ashore, except for breeding when they use rocky outcrops like this one. From the lighthouse I could see them both on the rock and also far out to sea where they flew in search of food. "I'll survive," I said again.

The man was on television again. Each news broadcast carried his picture and that of the dead villagers. The scenes were becoming padded out with maps and long distant shots of the surrounding mountains, but at the core of the broadcast, the man and his son remained. The man looked old, but was probably no older than me. Some of his teeth were missing in the front of his mouth and he had a deeply wrinkled face. He had a cut above one eye, but the roughness of the scab did not look too different from the rest of his skin. He stared intently at the camera as tears ran down his cheeks; only when the camera panned down to take a shot of the son did his head move to look at the small limp bundle in his arms. The son was lying flopped across his father's arms. One of the boy's legs dangled free, a rough dusty sandal on his foot. The boy's red and green shirt and loose red cotton trousers flapped gently in the air. The man blinked against the sun. He ended in silence, staring at the interviewer before turning to walk away from the camera, back into the house behind him.

Between writing my reports in the silence of my glass world and the television, I watched the birds, distant through my small round windows. I kept my binoculars by my side. Occasionally I picked them up to follow the individual birds that were many kilometres out to sea. I watched the silent white splashes appear on the surface of the sea as each bird dived into the gentle swell. They were more active than ever; the young birds were growing up and getting ready to leave. There is usually a lot of activity in the colony, but the movement was becoming intense. The large birds flew to find ever increasing amounts of food for their young. The adult birds spent all day out at sea; diving, flying, diving, flying. Then one day they would be gone.... North Africa, The Bay of Biscay, Iceland....places I had only ever seen on maps.

On the rock, the gannets and kittiwakes began to settle down to sit out the storm. There was less flying out to sea. Instead, they sat quietly and began to await the inevitable. They squeezed into small cracks and crevices to afford themselves a little protection. The adults still tried to give their young some warmth by wrapping their wings around them.

A few days ago, I saw a Roseate Tern. It just stopped for a rest then it was gone. God alone knows how far it had flown or where it was going. This island is not on its usual migratory route. My book described it as a very rare visitor to these coastal areas. So what drove a thing so small and so delicate to this rock? What lay in its sharp skull and behind its pin-bright eyes? It was sitting on the rail around the upper light and I simply moved across the window and it was gone. Presumably it had been knocked off course by the storm. But as the clouds gathered on the distant horizon it headed back towards them and the advancing veils and curtains of rain. I watched it through my window.

At school I used to listen only occasionally to Mr Mc Dermott, the teacher, when he told us about birds and wildlife. I would walk to school along the rough road and pay more attention to my games than the wildlife around me. Once Megan Leary pointed to a bird that was singing as it ascended in a series of bursts.

"There's a skylark," she said.

"Here's a right lark," I said pushing her.

Megan married Declan and moved away from the area before I did.

In my class at school, Mr McDermott had much better stories to tell. He told us about the Island of St. Kilda. He showed us a map of Scotland and pointed to somewhere out in the middle of the Atlantic or so it seemed to me. Then he told us about the people who used to live there: Simple and God-fearing he called them. I loved that phrase. He told us how they were removed from their homes and how the island became a military base. He told us how the islanders used to send and receive mail in a wooden box attached to an inflated sheep's bladder. The young men of St. Kilda would climb cliffs in their bare feet to get gull and kittiwake eggs for food. Before they were allowed to do this, they had to show their bravery by standing at the edge of a towering granite ledge in bare feet. Then they had to stand with only their heels on the rock, and finally they were to stand with only one heel on the rock with their other leg and their foot wavering out over the distant sea. Mr McDermott showed us photographs of the people of St. Kilda. They were small, almost fat people; perhaps they looked that way because of all the thick clothing they had to wear. Their beards were rough and unkempt. "Simple and God-fearing."

On the way home from school, Megan and her brother, James and I played at being on St. Kilda. James took off his shoes and tried to balance on one of his father's farm walls. At first he could not manage to balance on the rough granite blocks of the wall, but eventually he edged his toes out over the fresh air. With time, as the dusk drew in around us, he managed to balance on one heel, his foot half on and half off the wall. I could not do it and neither could Megan who was younger than us both. I satisfied myself by thinking that James would not have been able to balance on the rocks had they been a hundred metres high and not just one metre. As we walked to our respective homes, in the gloom I heard James shout, "King of St. Kilda."

The man appeared on the television again. The images hardly varied. Occasionally the order changed, but always the same message came across; he was at market so he missed the gas attack but all his family was killed, including his three year old son. He wished he was also dead. Some images, like these come to represent entire episodes of life, like the picture of the young naked girl running away from the bombing in the Vietnam war. Or the loyalist soldier being shot during the Spanish Civil War, his arms outstretched as if he was being crucified. Sometimes we live through important times.

There was world-wide reaction to the gassing. In a far-away building, the Ambassador of the man's country at the United Nations denied the gas attack and blamed the deaths on The Hand of God. He was surrounded by television cameras, microphones and jostling angry people. Outside the UN building a crowd of people was waving banners and placards. The man's role was reduced to a small cameo; we saw his tears and his dead child, but as we heard the voices of the newsreaders we saw other dead mothers and fathers and their children. They must have fallen just where they were when the gas hit them and only a few parents had a chance to cover their children. Some groups of bodies lay next to games or books spread out on the dirt road outside the houses. Others were in the corners of courtyards around unfinished meals. The people from outlying villages arrived to bury their relatives and friends. Those that had not been buried were covered with blankets. And still the man came onto each broadcast crying and wishing he were dead.

I ventured out onto the rock. I had been busy but I tried to get out at least once each day. Walking carefully amongst the birds so as not to disturb them, I passed through a slowly moving lawn of white; like a silk sheet rippling. The birds barely acknowledged my presence, but simply ruffled their feathers and fidgeted on their rough nesting mounds. I walked the hundred or so metres to the end of the rock and looked out over the to the west. Above the line of the horizon, I saw the first few clouds that formed the leading edge of the storm. There, just beyond my view, was the storm that knocked the tern off course as it tried to find its directions in the maelstrom. In the evening glow I tried to bring myself to stand on the edge of the rock, with my toes out over the ocean. Below me was a ten metre drop into the water. I didn't do it. Instead, I turned and walked back amongst the birds.

When I returned to the lighthouse the radio was crackling.

"Where have you been?" asked the voice when I picked up the receiver.

"Nowhere."

"We've been trying for ten minutes."

"Sorry."

"Shall we come and get you."

"No. I'm fine."

The next morning, I walked to the top of the lighthouse to watch the clouds gathering. Then I went through my routine and checked the systems. The radio receiver I was upgrading was to be controlled by a single computer; one station would handle over fifteen lights along this coast. I just needed to be present as it was re-tested for the first time.

As the first specks of rain began to fall I went down the steps and out onto the rock. The wind was growing. The birds were adjusting themselves to meet the storm head on. The younger birds were being protected by their parents whilst the older chicks settled down alongside the adults. I was about half-way along the rock when, almost without notice, the wind and rain hit the rock hard. I turned around to return to the light, but before I closed the door into the storm I looked back over the colony to see the birds squatting and crouching close to the rock. Back in my office, I watched them through the window.

Mr. McDermott told us of the storms on St. Kilda. Of how the boats could not put to sea for weeks, sometimes months. The whole Atlantic Ocean would seem to hurl itself at the small granite island and the islanders could only sit and wait. He read us accounts of the storms, of the islands and how whole herds of sheep were moved from island to island to graze the scarce grass. During storms the sheep could die of starvation if left for too long on small islands where there was too little food. Or they would be washed off the islands by the large waves and their bodies would float, rotting and bloated, between the islands. The storms, he said, were the reasons that the authorities gave for the removal of people from the islands. But, Mr. Mc Dermott said that it was really because they wanted the island for a military base. So Mr. McDermott's grand-parents were shipped off the island and were given a home in Glasgow. He had a photograph of the tall tenement block in which his ancestors lived and, only five months after arriving off St. Kilda, died.

"They couldn't take it, you see," he said as we stared at the crumpled photo.

"And I end up teaching you lot," he would always say, smiling again. At the end of each term, as a special treat, he would tell us stories of St. Kilda.

Through the storm the television images moved on. They still showed the man, but also the remaining villagers from surrounding areas packing up their belongings and moving down the hillside into the rocky valley floor. They said that they were moving together for safety. They sat in family groups in the bare countryside. Tents were being flown in from around the world and they clung, with their occupants, to the rocks and scree. Simple and God-fearing people. Occasionally the sound disappeared from the television, so the man's voice came and went. The storm raged outside my room, silencing the man's sorrow. The hills where the people gathered were bare and dusty and the sun cast deep shadows in the valleys. The people sat motionless outside their tents on the pale stones as the camera panned across their faces. The reporter then stood facing the camera to tell us that the refugees would need to be moved to safer and more suitable ground far away from their homes as the mountains could not sustain them for very long. He told us that the valleys were inaccessible for the rescue services and international aid. And, finally, the man appeared again, holding the body of his young son.

As the storm subsided after many hours, I once again looked out onto the rock below. The groups of birds were bedraggled and weather-beaten; lying and crouching together with the young moving as close to their parents as possible. I watched both the television and the storm until the rain and wind finally abated. When it did so, I went down the steps and onto the shining rock once more. Many of the birds were badly injured, and a lot were dead. Others were just in shock. But already they were starting to get on with their lives. Some were flying off to sea again to seek the food for their young.

At the end of the rock, I stared down into the muddied waters. The storm had stirred up sand and seaweed and clouded the normally clear sea. It moved aggressively some distance below me. I sat on the edge with my feet dangling into space beneath me. I moved my legs from side to side to the rhythm of the waves, tapping my heels against the rock. After several minutes I stood up and took off my shoes. I moved slowly towards the edge of the cliff. For a short time I waited about a metre back from the drop but then I shuffled, a few centimetres, at a time, until my toes were at the absolute edge of the rock. Then I manoeuvred my feet timidly until the toes were over the edge. I moved on until half of each foot was sticking out over the rock; I rested only on my heels. Then I lifted one foot and stretched it out in front of me. I stood with only one heel on the rock with the rest of me suspended in space over the sea. I looked towards the horizon from which the storm came and towards which the tern flew. I looked from side to side at the confusion and sorrow around me in the colony until my calf-muscles ached. Then, I slowly stepped back from the edge. I put my shoes and socks on and returned to the lighthouse. The birds were quite still and subdued as I moved amongst them. Back in the lighthouse I answered the radio.

"We're coming to get you."

"I'm alright."

"We're coming to get you. How are things ?"

"Nothing changes."

"We'll send a boat."

"I'm not going anywhere," I said.

So now, for the last time, I sit at my desk and through the small window I see the birds. More of them are venturing out to sea again. I pick up my binoculars and follow them. I look down also at the birds still sitting on their nest sites. I look at those that are injured and at those that have been killed by the storm. Their bodies lie in strange, contorted shapes, their necks badly twisted. I think to myself, "The Hand of God."

From time to time I turn my binoculars towards the headland. After about half an hour a small boat emerges from behind it. Beyond it, and oddly out of proportion because of the binoculars, rises the cliff; thirty, forty, fifty metres in a vertical climb. I imagine myself standing barefoot at the top of that cliff; The King of St. Kilda.

The boat moves slowly through the open water. It will take an hour and a half, possibly two, to reach me. It moves carefully through the swell which is still high after the winds. Once it is clear of the cliffs, it turns towards the lighthouse, towards the island and the calm which is all that remains of the storm.

Lost

My wife read out the names like a Requiem. Vimy Ridge, The Somme, Arras. She moved her finger further to the east on the map and read more names: Verdun, Mort-Homme, Vauquois.

"We should go and look at some of these places," she said, looking out at the landscape that flickered in the sunshine.

"Maybe on the way back" I said.

She opened the guidebook as we drove along the French auto-route. She read aloud about the start of the Battle of the Somme. "Listen to this," she said. "On the first day of the battle there were 57,000 British casualties alone." She turned over the page. "In the four months of the onslaught there were 415,000 British, 195,000 French and over 600,000 German casualties"

"It's hard to imagine what made them all just keep going," I said. "All that for a few hundred yards of mud." I chose my words carefully. I did not want to upset our delicate balance and I was comforted by the topic of our conversation. Its neutrality allowed us to talk without the usual bickering.

She left my remark unanswered and read a further extract from the guidebook. She finished by saying again that we really should go and visit some of the graves and battlefields.

"On the way home, perhaps," I said. "I thought we'd agreed that we would get further south for the first night."

Her response was instant.

"You just can't take things as they come, can you? You can't do that one thing for me? We're on holiday for God's sake."

The moment had left us. She picked up the map again. "Why don't we just bloody well drive all the way there in one go? And then get home as quick as we can?" she said. She turned to face out of her window. With the map across her knees, she stared out towards the fields that flowed in gentle waves out to the horizon.

We had agreed to come on this break to spend time together. Time with no distractions, away from the normal pressures. We'd been spending our days niggling at each other without resolving anything or getting anywhere. It surprised me how close to the surface the bickering lay. Every time it broke out, it was over what to me seemed trivial issues. It had been going on for months. We had, I thought, planned to drive as far south as Dijon on the first day, well south of the battlefields.

"Where is the Vimy Ridge from here?" I asked. I was looking for the threads of our previous conversation.

She gestured vaguely to the right and said, "Over there somewhere." The landscape passed calmly outside the window.

I shuffled awkwardly in the driver's seat, and changed the position of my hands. I raised and lowered my shoulders to relieve some of the stiffness, but also to let her witness my discomfort. In the corner of my eye I saw her watching me. I rolled my head and neck slowly and, as I turned my head to stretch, I saw through the windscreen a canal which ran beneath the auto-route. It was dark green, almost choked with weed. Through the thick gel a small motor-boat chugged away from us. In it, two men sat facing each other as they cut slowly through the dappled light. I motioned towards them with a brief nod of my head.

"That's the life," I said, still searching for a no-man's land for the conversation "I wonder where they're heading."

"Perhaps they've got to get a lot further south by this evening," she said.

"Oh Fuck Off."

We drove for several minutes in silence. We passed a town perched unrealistically on a hill-top in the distance; the twin towers of the large church looking out around the surrounding plain. There was an industrial town on the horizon, smoke from several chimneys drifting aimlessly in the still heat. A sign on the side of the road gave distances to cities spread out across Europe. The names were northern: Brussels, Strasbourg, Frankfurt. Cities stretching like beacons along the unknown highways of the continent.

It did not feel right though. Dijon was not mentioned and neither were the cities further south; the ones we would pass on the long road to the Mediterranean. I did not say anything until after we passed another sign at a junction when I had to break the silence. I told her I thought we had taken a wrong turn and asked whether she knew where we were.

"I don't know." she said, and picked up the map.

We could not remember the town that was named on the last junction, so we had to wait for the next one. At the sign she quickly consulted the map; we'd missed an interchange and we were on the wrong part of the auto-route, heading east, not south.

"Shit," I said. "Why didn't you say"

"Because I didn't know, that's why."

"You've got the map."

"Oh...and you're not driving, are you not?"

I turned off at the next junction. We paid to go through the toll-barrier and came to a large new roundabout where I stopped. There was no other traffic around. The mid-day sun was piercing and the car engine idled and the fan started-up. The plants in the middle of the roundabout were already beginning to wilt and die from the drought. There were some pieces of machinery parked on the freshly seeded verge with a few unset kerbstones lying around, but there were no signs around the bare circle of the roundabout. There was nothing to help us make our way. I looked out of the back window.

"This is a new interchange. It's not on the map," she said.

"Let me see," I said taking the map.

"We can't get back on from here."

"Shit."

"Will you stop saying that?"

I drove along the only other open road off the roundabout. A new dual carriageway was being constructed and in the distance heavy machinery was working. Our road, though, was narrow and lined with an avenue of tall poplar trees. When I could see beyond them, the fields rose and flowed away from us in shallow steps and fleetingly I thought of the thousands of men who, in a different world, struggled up each small hill, only to arrive at the next one and if they were lucky the one beyond that. And endless terrain of struggle. I tried to envisage 10,000 people, then 57,000 and 600,000.

We drove through their landscape for nearly ten minutes before we reached a town where, as we passed the nameplate, she picked up the map to locate us. I pulled off the road into the market square and she handed me the opened sheet. "We're here," she said, pointing a long way to the east of where we should have been.

"Shit." I looked at the map, quickly trying to work out how long the delay would be. "We could eat here," I said after a while.

She opened the car door and got out without replying.

A small knot of men was sitting under one of the trees that lined the square. They watched us get out. My wife lifted her rucksack out of the car. It was a small black leather one that I remember her buying the previous year. When she bought it, she'd explained it away by saying that it was much more sensible, much more practical than a handbag. But she still asked me whether it made her appear as if she was trying to look like a student. "Mutton dressed as lamb?" she'd asked. I told her that it didn't, which was the truth, but I didn't tell her that I thought she looked beautiful. I cannot say those things anymore.

She put on her rucksack and pulled her sunglasses down over her eyes. The way that she did it reminded me of the reasons I fell in love with her. Yes, she is beautiful; she still looks attractive as she adjusts her bag and glasses and brushes the front of her tee shirt to straighten it; the confidence with which she walks ahead of me in this small French town.

When we met, we used to lie in bed talking on weekend mornings when there was no work. I was desperate then for her to love me like I felt I loved her. But she would never say. She said that if I wanted to know how she really felt, I should look into her eyes, so I spent those early days doing just that, looking for signs. Perhaps I should have told her more things then.

I walked behind her and watched the men beneath the tree looking at her as she moved down the street. Most of the shops that we passed were dark and empty. They were closed for lunchtime. There were no cafés or restaurants in sight. I followed her for a while before asking:

"Where are we going?"

"I don't know. You said we could eat here."

"It was just an idea."

Further along the main street, turning into another lane, we found a small café and went in. It was empty. She tipped her sunglasses up onto her forehead again and walked over to the counter. She picked up a menu and looked at it for a short while before tossing it almost dismissively back onto the counter. She went over to a table by the window. Taking her bag off and hanging it over her chair, she sat down.

"Is this OK?" I asked, sitting opposite her.

"It's fine" she said, turning to look out of the window.

We ate in comparative silence, the gentle scraping of the cutlery being the loudest noise. We edged around subjects. I asked her what she wanted to do when we finally reached the south coast. She was not bothered, she said, she just wanted to relax. Did she want to go to Marseille or St Tropez? She couldn't decide now. At the end of the meal, we were no clearer on our plans and had made no progress, but we had not argued.

Each time the old woman who was serving us came in we stopped talking as she smiled at us and served us our food and coffee. But on one occasion she patted my wife on the arm as she spoke to her and gave her a longer smile, then she looked over at me and, still smiling, gave me a little nod, although I did not know what she had said. I smiled back.

When we stood up to leave, the owner came over to us again and clasped both my wife's hands in hers as she spoke to us in French. She switched her gaze from my wife to me and back again. When she let go of her hands, the woman patted my wife on both cheeks with her rough palms.

"What was all that about?" I asked as we left.

"I don't know."

"She kept using the word love...amour."

"She doesn't know the half of it."

Outside, many shops were still closed and the houses had blinds pulled down for the lunchtime break. The sun was still pouring across the sky and we ambled along in the brightness. My wife pulled her sunglasses down over her eyes again.

All the windows were shuttered and guarded so I could not see in.

We tried to retrace our steps back to the car. As I walked behind her, I noticed a hair on the back of her tee shirt. I thought about removing it; I even raised my hand to pick it off, but lowered it again without touching her. Eventually, we ended up on a street neither of us recognised so we doubled back and found ourselves tangled in a web of streets that, to us, had no defining features. Each turn brought us to another junction and just another set of choices.

"We must be heading in the right direction," I said.

"Probably."

"There's a limit to how lost we can get."

"You'd have thought so."

We reached another turning. To the left was a road sign that showed the way back to the auto-route. I pointed it out and said we needed to remember how to get out and on our way again. She simply looked up at the sign then turned to the right, towards where we assumed the car would be. I caught her up and tried to hold her hand. We let them rest together for a while, but then they drifted apart so we walked side by side back to the car in silence.

In the square, the men had gone and ours was the only car remaining. Before getting in I went over to the war memorial. It was a simple stone column, set on a series of stepped pedestals. On top of the column was a bronze statue of a French Infantryman. The front of the monument bore the single message "A nos morts." Down each side, there were rows and rows of names. I circled the base to look at all four sides. Certain surnames were repeated over and over. The sheer number of people from this small village who died in the First World War swept over me like a tide; entire generations removed forever. And again fleetingly I imagined lists like these reaching towards infinity until a million names had been accounted for.

"Do you want to look around here?" I asked as I unlocked the car.

"Like where? Everywhere is shut."

"I mean some of the battlefields." I tried to remember the places she mentioned that were near there. "The Somme? Arras?"

"It doesn't matter. You want to get on."

We got into the car. I switched on the fan and let the air cool for a while before starting the engine. As I pulled out into the road, she asked me if I wanted her to drive.

"I'm alright for now," I said. "I might get you to drive later, though." We had a long way to go.

I followed the road looking for the sign back onto the auto-route.

Out of town, we eventually rejoined the motorway and after an hour reached the missed junction for the road south. She pointed to the signs above us that indicated which lane we should be in.

"Here, the inside lane...we don't want to mess up again," she said.

I indicated to take the turning for Dijon, Avignon and the south; aware like her that we might only briefly be emerging from the landscape of some distant conflict.

Exile

That afternoon George West hit his daughter.

It wasn't a gentle tap like he used when his children were toddlers and he and his wife dragged them round the shopping-mall. His daughter was fifteen now; a slap like that would have no effect.

No, he hit his daughter hard across the face.

Afterwards, as he stared into the bareness of his empty wardrobe with the metal hangers echoing sparsely on the rail, he rubbed his hand which still throbbed from the blow. He had already packed his bag.

Later, he sat in the waiting-room at the train station, still rubbing his hand. At his feet was the small bag with his clothes in it.

George West stood up and moved over to the window of the waiting-room to look out onto the darkening station. Dull lights on each platform lapped at the edges of the gloom. All of the kiosks were closed and boarded with metal shutters. He could not see anyone else around; the loud-speaker was silent. He went out and looked at the overhead monitor on the platform that gave departure times. His train, the one taking him to his sister's house, left at nine-thirty; in twenty minutes.

Checking again along the platform, he returned to sit down in the waiting-room.

He tried to remember the details of what had happened. His daughter had said, "And what the fuck do you know, anyway?" It was then that he raised his hand and hit his own daughter. He had watched Julie's face turn from the impact and her long, brown pony-tail flare out behind her. He had seen the blood appear at the corner of his daughter's mouth and he had heard the intake of Julie's breath as she began to cry.

His own daughter had called him a bastard and said, "And what the fuck do you know, anyway?" And in that instant - it had probably been no more than a second, possibly less - many thoughts had crossed his mind, but the one that he acted on was that he decided to hit her; on such choices the world turns, he thought.

They had both stood in shock as her screams subsided and it was in that silent moment George West had also decided he had to leave.

When a young couple came into the waiting-room he was startled because he'd seen no-one around and his thoughts had been lost in the past.

The pair bustled into the room, carrying on talking as if they were alone. Surely they must have seen him, or maybe he'd become invisible as well.

"You can't smoke in here, Carl," said the woman. She was wearing tight jeans tucked into boots and a tee shirt like George West's daughter might wear. She had blonde hair extensions. The man also wore denims, a checked shirt and some trainers. They were about twenty, he guessed. He was carrying a large hold-all, but all she had was a small handbag.

She wobbled slightly on her high heeled boots.

"Well I don't want to bloody well smoke," said the man. As he spoke he turned around and stopped right in front of the girl's face, nodding his head violently from side to side to emphasise each word. "You are *always* fucking going on about things, you...*aren't* you?"

The young woman stepped around him, eyes down, and sat on the other side of the waiting room from George West; the man sat down, but did not take the seat next to her, sitting instead a few seats away. "There's always fucking *something*, isn't there?" he said as he sat, as if remembering something new and important to say. He ran his hand over his shaved head and George West saw that he had the word 'love' tattooed across his knuckles.

The air around him bristled.

He leaned forward and stared ahead turning his mobile phone around in his hands while the girl looked at him across the empty seats.

"What now?" he said, looking up to catch her watching him.

"I just thought you might like a smoke, that's all."

"Jesus fucking Christ, give it a rest." He looked at his hands as he spoke, continuing to turn his phone over and over. George West saw the word 'hate' tattooed on the other hand.

At that moment, the woman's mobile began to ring. It was a tune George West recognised from his daughter's radio. The woman flicked open the phone.

"Hiya," she said, then turning to the man, said "It's our Lynette...I'm just telling Carl it's you." The man stood up and told the girl he was going out to look at the train times. "He's just going to look at the train times. Yeah, we're at the station.

No, it's not here yet. How's it going? Will you meet us? Yeah.... Yeah...Right. No, he's not back yet. I'll call you on the train. See you soon, Darling." And she flicked the phone closed.

For the first time since they'd arrived, the young woman acknowledged George West.

"It's my sister," she said, waving her phone. "She's getting married. We're going to visit her."

"I see," said George West

"Carl's just checking the train times."

"Right."

"Where are you going?"

"To see my sister," said George West.

"No way. Isn't that weird?"

The man came back into the waiting room; he had a cigarette in his hand and exhaled smoke as he entered. "The train's on time, Babe," he said. His air of menace had dissolved for the moment.

"This man's going to see his sister, too," said the woman.

"Is that right?"

The man sat down next to the young woman and put his arm around her shoulders and kissed her on the side of the head. She wriggled away from him, embarrassed. She mouthed something to him that George West thought must have been about him watching them, but the man lifted the hem of her tee shirt and put his hand on her bare stomach. He began to move it up towards her breasts as he winked and then stared hard at George West. The young woman laughed and moved his hand away, so he leaned back, still looking at George West.

"Where does your sister live, then?" he asked across the room, taking a pull on his cigarette. A hand, the one saying love, reached down to rest on his groin, his legs spread as he lounged back in the hard plastic chair.

"Liverpool."

"That's where your Lynette lives, isn't it, Babe?"

"God, yeah. We're both seeing our sisters in Liverpool. That's so weird. Do you believe in fate? I do. I think everything's planned out, me. Don't you?"

They all let the thought hang in the air unanswered.

The man tapped his trainers on the ground and the young woman looked at the front of her mobile phone as if willing it to ring. George West stared across the room at them. After several minutes of the silence, broken only by the tapping of the man's feet, the young woman with the cropped tee-shirt stood up and straightened her clothes with a couple of brushes of her hand. She stumbled to one side as she rose. George West reckoned that they had both been drinking.

"I'm just going to check the train time," she said.

"I just looked, Babe," said the man, stopping the tapping of his feet.

"Well, I'm bored." Her boots clacked across the floor of the waiting room and echoed around the bare walls. As the door clicked shut behind her the strip light in the waiting room flickered. After a short silence, the man spoke.

"Her sister's mad," he said.

"Is she?" said George West.

"Too right....Fucking mental. She wants to marry this bloke who's twice her age."

"Perhaps she loves him. Some people do love each other."

"Loves his money more like. Some things are just not right, don't you think? And him. He just wants to get his leg over with some young bit of fluff. Would you like it if it was your daughter? No....me neither. Some things just shouldn't happen...don't you think, Babe? Some things are just not right?" The young woman had come back into the waiting room. "I was just saying that some things are not right."

"I don't know what you're on about." The young woman stood at the door.

"Your sister marrying that bloke."

"That's up to her...them." She looked over at George West as she walked towards her seat "That's up to her isn't it?"

"I imagine it is," said George West.

"Whatever...the train's on time," said the young woman as she sat down next to the man.

"I could have told you that, Babe."

"I was just telling him," she said, pointing at George West.

The man leaned forward, threw his cigarette on the floor and rubbed it out with his foot.

"Well don't expect me to go to the fucking wedding, that's all," he said, arms resting on his knees.

George West stood up and walked towards the door. "I need some air," he said as he opened the door feeling that he ought to explain himself before he left. He picked up his bag on the way.

Out on the platform, the night air was cold and clear. His breath clung like mist round his face. He hunted in his coat pockets for some gloves. The ones he had with him were cheap, striped woollen ones. His daughter had bought them for him a couple of years ago; he remembered opening the present on his birthday, feigning delight at the odd choice.

But that had been his role, hadn't it? Trying to keep everyone happy, making sure their lives rubbed along together.

He put the gloves on and saw that some of his fingers

poked out from the ends of the gloves where the wool had worn away; he'd buy a new pair when he got to his sister's house. He took the rest of the contents out of his pocket. There was his wallet, with its few notes and coins, photographs of the family, his house keys, the train tickets and a receipt from his last trip to the chemist for the happy-pills he now remembered leaving on the bedside table when he crept out that evening. That was probably a good thing, he was sure the pills made him worse.

George West returned the things to his coat pocket.

Walking slowly up and down the platform, he passed the waiting room, looking in at the couple each time. First they were sitting down, the woman talking at the man whilst he stared ahead. The next time, he was standing staring out of the window smoking another cigarette while she read a magazine behind him. With each pass, their positions changed like photographs. The room looked warm, but George West did not want to go back in. He liked the clear sharp night air; he had found the smokiness and edginess of the couple constricting. He couldn't breathe. He needed the fresh air to think.

Because, what the fuck *did* he know, anyway?

He could have listed many things for his daughter. He'd had a life too; one which didn't involve work or families or trying to keep the peace at home. One which remained invisible to his children. But what could he say he *knew*? He had experienced many things: pain, frustration, the sheer bloody magic of seeing your children being born, and what it feels like to fail them. Happy, sad. He'd seen it all.

But what George West knew now was that it wasn't all

planned out for us and there were choices in this world which were always there, flowing under the surface like water under ice. Husbands hit their wives, men hit children, and yes women hit-out too. And now, he'd chosen to break something that could never be repaired and it was him who had to leave. *That's* what the fuck he knew.

His train arrived. As it passed, he looked into each carriage and constructed small cosy lives around the people in the windows. Couples going home from visiting friends, people going out for the evening, women finishing a day's shopping. People going home from work. Girls' days out, gangs of blokes out on the drink. The whole mundane world, in all its beauty, was passing him by.

When the brakes screeched, took hold and the train slowed, he looked at his own image in the windows. He saw a tired person - an older one than he remembered – wearing a dull overcoat and faded trousers. His thinning hair hung apologetically around his face. He tried to imagine what the people on the train would think about him as they saw him standing on the platform with his small holdall. Did he look as if he had just rushed out of the house? Did he look ill or as if he had been crying? Why was a middle-aged man travelling alone so late in the evening with only a few belongings? George West closed his eyes rather than look at his own image any longer.

He moved to the nearest carriage door and pressed the button for it to open. It hissed and slid back as the couple emerged from the waiting room. The man ran with the bag over his shoulder and the young woman ran as best she could in her high heels.

"Come on, Babe," he shouted.

"Don't let it go without me, Carl."

George West got on quickly and sat at a table-seat where a woman and what he assumed was her grand-daughter were already sitting; he did not want the young couple to join him. The woman and the grand-daughter were both in the window seats, so he sat next to the little girl, who did not turn round from looking outside. The woman was reading a newspaper and George West saw her eyes flicker briefly over the top of the paper as she looked to see who was sitting down at their table. The carriage smelled of damp clothes.

The train did not move. A woman's voice from further down the carriage asked what the hold-up was.

"I don't fucking know do I, Babe?" came the man's voice.

"Well, we needn't have rushed."

The woman at the table tutted and the young girl turned to see where the voices were coming from, then kneeled on the seat and leaned to put her face against the window again. She pressed her nose even closer to the window to look past the platform to the street-lights and the houses beyond.

"Look at all the Christmas trees in those flats," she said happily to her grandmother.

"Don't shout," said her grandmother without looking up from the newspaper.

"I'm not shouting."

"You were."

"But look at them all."

"Why don't you count them." Again the woman did not look up. The girl began to count them out- loud. "Do it in your head," snapped her grandmother. "People don't want to hear your voice. There's too much shouting as it is." This time she looked back along the carriage then briefly made eye contact with George West.

The little girl started to count the Christmas trees again, pointing at them with her finger as if she didn't want to miss any of them. The window glistened with small drops of rain and reflected some of the dull station-lights on to the little girl's face.

And as he watched her count the trees, George West felt the girl was becoming part of the brightness outside the window; sparkling like the lights she was counting. He remembered similar bright pin-pricks of joy from his own daughter, when she was younger; from a time when George West could have imagined they would grow up to be friends.

The train finally began to move and the girl was jolted by the motion, falling against George West who, without thinking, held out his hand to stop the girl falling further. The grandmother looked up and he quickly removed his hand. The little girl did not look to see who was supporting her, but leaned back and again pressed her face against the glass to see the tower-block for as long as she could. George West watched her lips move as she continued to count the bright trees of light in her head.

"Twenty two...twenty three...twenty four," she mouthed. And George West, following the girl's gaze towards the tower block as the train moved, also counted the Christmas trees inside his head. "Twenty five...twenty six...twenty seven..." until he could no longer see them to count.

The little girl sat down and looked across the table at her grandmother, her face full of expectation, wanting the woman to ask her how many there were; how many shiny trees had she seen in the brooding flats? And what were all the boys and girls getting for Christmas, did she think? But the woman was silent. And as he looked at the little girl, then back at the buildings outside, George West recognised again the deep loneliness that is to be found in families.

Then as the train picked up speed, he watched the tower-block receding, getting smaller and smaller. Disappearing to nothing but a few specks of light as they moved further and further into the dark.

Sick Bed

I peered through the crack between the door and the door-frame. I could see my naked father; he was standing in front of my mother next to the bed. I swayed gently from side to side to see more. Through the narrow view into their private world I could see the crude hairs on his back nearly reaching his pale buttocks. Skin hung loosely on his arms and thighs. Rays of early morning sunlight picked out dust in the air.

He moved aside to adjust the bedroom curtains, revealing my naked mother, her small almost hairless body curved and delicate in comparison. The glimpse was only brief because my father returned to stand in front of her, the room now darker. I saw her hands appear from around his waist as she hugged him, then they moved down his coarse back to rest on his hips.

The last thing I saw was my mothers' legs raise as they sat, almost fell onto the bed and I heard the springs creak loudly to receive their weight, after which I could only hear their soft moans and whisperings.

I turned to go back to my room and the floorboards let out a gentle squeal and I felt the silence from my parents' room swell around me until it filled the whole house. I stood still. They called out my name.

"Col.....Col......is that you?"

I remained silent, my heart the only thing I could hear, until their murmurings started once more and I returned to my room. There I pulled the sheets and blankets over my head to try to block out the light and the noise and the images of their bedroom.

My father is upstairs alone in that bed now. He is old and ill. Each tiny stroke drives him down further. He will not recover from this long slow descent into nothingness. From the kitchen, I hear him banging with his walking stick on the floorboards above my head. I let a few moments pass before I respond, shouting that I will soon be there, but I wait for another few minutes before I go up.

I stand at the foot of the bed looking at its peeling padded headboard, the wallpaper behind it torn where it has rubbed against the wall for so long. The floral-patterned paper in the rest of the room is faded from many years of sunlight. My mother told me she gave birth to me in this bed with my father smoking in the next room. And now my father lies in it, still. I look at the small frail mound of the bedspread which delineates his aging body.

"Where have you been?" he asks.

"I was doing something."

"It must have been important."

"Have you taken your pills?"

"Of course," he says.

"I'm only asking you."

"I'm only telling you."

"You banged on the floor; what do you want?" I say.

He falls silent, as he often does having got me upstairs. Eventually, I leave the room, after opening the small window.

I do not want an argument now. But I have barely reached the top of the stairs before he starts calling me in his thin breathy voice.

"What is it?" I return to the room.

"I want the window closed."

I look out of the window as I pull it shut. Down in the street, quiet now in mid-morning, there are few people around. Our neighbour is out on the road as usual, washing his old car. The only other people are two women from a couple of doors down walking to do their weekly shop. I watch them for a while before turning back to him.

"Is there anything else?" I ask before I go.

Back in the kitchen, I turn on the radio. I sit with a mug of tea, cupped between my hands. On the draining board, the washing up from breakfast is still stacked. A single pan, a cup and one plate. Through the window, a small breeze shakes the tree out on the street. It is beginning to rain.

On one trip years ago, many months after I had seen them naked, I held their hands tightly as we dashed through rain up the steps at the front of the museum. We ran blustering into the front foyer and the attendant smiled as we shook our coats and my mother folded her umbrella. We entered the main hall where tall metal pillars pulled my eyes up into the roof. It was as big as a temple. Black balconies of painted wrought iron ran around the hall with doorways leading off into vast rooms full of wonder. We asked the man for the ancient Egyptian collection. He pointed towards the stairs, gave us a gallery number then touched his cap to my mother and smiled again. On the next level and through several doors, I finally stood at the first of the rooms which I was looking for. The small plaque said, *Ancient Egypt*. It was tip-toe quiet.

In the first two rooms there were pieces of pottery and brooches. This was not what I wanted. In the third room, though, there were huge displays looming large and powerful under the bright spot-lights. There were big stone coffins behind ropes that were strung out to stop people getting too close. Paintings on the walls depicted pyramids and gangs of people pulling blocks of stone. Around the room, wooden casks stood as big as my mother's wardrobe and there, in the middle of the room, was the biggest cask of all painted in gold, and black and blue containing the mummified remains of an ancient king. This was what I wanted to see.

My parents followed on behind me, my mother's small feet tapping through the silence. She stood next to me in this room; my room, surrounded by the enormity of the ancient dead. I walked round the cask and imagined the king's world ending in the tight confines of that wooden box. Did they really bury them alive, I asked. And where did they get the stone for the pyramids? And did they pull their brains out through their noses before they buried them? Were they really only four feet high? I asked so many questions that my parents could not answer....

I ask my father, "Shall I close the curtains?" I am in his room again.

"Yes...no..." he pauses.

"So that you can sleep?"

There is no response. Even our silences are now coiled tight with the tension of what can no longer be said between us. I wait for him to speak, but instead he closes his eyes and pretends to be asleep. He uses the silences as the only power he has, and as I look down at him, frustrated, I try not to despise his weak body, his bones jutting-out like coat hangers beneath the covers and what he has become.

I get up to close the curtains anyway, then lean over him to re-arrange the pillows so he looks more comfortable. As I let his head slowly back down he moans slightly; there is a small stain of food at the corner of his mouth and the veins on his cheeks are broken, like frost on a window.

"I'm going back down."

There is silence.

"Is there anything else?"

Again, silence.

"I'll be downstairs."

Instead of answering, he starts to move and tries to swing his feet out of the bed. I watch him struggle for a few seconds before speaking.

"What are you doing?"

"I need to go to the toilet."

"Why didn't you say?"

"I didn't want to bother you."

"Jesus Christ, Dad..."

I move in front of him, and let his frail hands wrap around my fingers, then I watch as he swings his legs out from under the covers. Sticking out from his pyjama trousers, they are thin and hairless. He gets into an upright position and we shuffle towards the bathroom with me facing him as I move backwards. Like this, we cannot avoid each other's eyes and this is the most uncomfortable part.

When we have got to the bathroom, I leave him and return to his room to wait for him sitting on his bed. It smells of sweat, of his ointment and of a weakening life. His dressing table surface is now full of bottles of pills, bottles of mineral water and cream for his bedsores and chapped skin. Once, it gleamed with my mother's perfume and jewellery; her mirror-backed hairbrush sitting on a lace doily. Now it is dusty and covered in the trappings of illness.

As I wait for my father, I stare back at myself in the mirror and bounce gently on the bed remembering the evening after we returned from the museum. I took the sheet off my parents' big double bed and wrapped it around me pretending to be an Egyptian king. I jumped on to their bed then walked backwards and forwards, watching myself in the mirror, imagining myself as a king, with enormous pyramids being built for me; an epic leader of the whole world.

A hero.

My imaginings then were brought to an abrupt end by my mother's gentle chiding telling me to get ready for bed. Now, when the headboard bangs slightly on the wall behind as I bounce, it is my father's voice from the bathroom that stops me.

"What are you doing?".

"Nothing."

"I'm ready now."

"I'm coming."

We shuffle back to his room, him with his head bowed and me looking emptily ahead trying not to make eye contact. When he is back in bed, he lies down and I leave him to go downstairs and wait for his health visitor.

She is a young woman who breezes into the house with a bright smile and the smell of happiness. She looks like she has just stepped out of a shower, so fresh and eager. I stand awkwardly with her in the entrance before taking her coat and hanging it up.

"How are things?" she asks as I lead her upstairs.

"The usual." And I laugh in a forced way, conscious of my shallow reply. "We get through."

In my father's room, she goes straight to the window to open the curtains then sits him upright and chats to him. I stand un-needed in the background, trying to listen to what she is telling him; watching my father come to life with her chirping conversation. Before she starts to examine him, she goes to wash her hands.

While she is in the bathroom he struggles to sit more comfortably and as I help he motions towards the corridor with his eyes.

"She's a cracker, eh?"

"She's pretty."

"You should ask her out."

"Don't be daft."

It is in brief moments like this that I think we could still be friends and have some fun in our lives, but I know it is too late; the sickness has removed that hope. He is only animated now because she is here. I can no longer coax the fun from him like the nurse. So I end up washing him and taking him to the toilet and feeding him in between going to work; what does my love add up to, anyway, but looking after him? He can't ask me to be his friend as well, can he?

"She's coming back. Now's your chance," he says. "I was just telling our Col here that a pretty girl like you wouldn't mind being asked out," he says to the nurse as she comes in.

"Maybe when you feel a bit better," she jokes, smiling at him. Then turning to me she adds, "I'll be here a while. Why don't you go and get a breath of fresh air. You must have things to do." Her face is momentarily serious.

"Probably," I say.

I tell them I am going to have a shower before I go out to get a paper. I briefly listen to them laughing along the corridor before I let the water flow over me until the sensation and the noise drown out their voices and there is a kind of silence.

The bed, too, has been part of *my* life.

One of my girlfriends wore long, dark cheese-cloth dresses and Doc Martins. Her hair was dyed with henna and she wore patchouli oil. She even got me to wear it. She was as near as I came to rebelling.

"What's that smell?" my mother asked when my girlfriend was round once.

"Patchouli oil."

"Smells like something died."

"I like it."

"You would," she said.

Eventually, my girlfriend avoided my parents and came round when they were not there. On one occasion, she began to look round the house, leaving me alone in the sitting room watching television. After a while, she shouted for me to come upstairs. I looked for her and eventually found her in my parents' room, lying on the bed.

"Let's have sex here." she said.

"What are you doing? They'll kill me."

"Come on. They'll never know."

"You're sick. This is my parents' bed."

"Come on Col. Let's shag." She sensed the awkwardness and leaned heavily on the words. "Come on. Let's *shag.*"

As I moved closer to her, she pulled me down, and started to kiss me. For a moment, in the deep musky folds of the patchouli oil, I felt myself drifting towards making love on their bed. She started to unbutton my shirt, but I pulled back.

"No. Let's go to my room."

"It's too small."

So we got up, and I straightened the eiderdown. Although we didn't make love, she still left the smell of excitement and sex in my life and in my parents' room. The room that now smells of ointment and staleness and the minutiae of my father's slow death.

Before I leave I go in to say goodbye to the nurse and my father and ask if there is anything that they want. The nurse turns to smile and say no thanks.

"You look tired," she says.

"I'll be OK."

"Your father's great company today," she says. "Take your time."

I walk down the street. It is now early afternoon, there is a slight drizzle in the air, but I like that; the rain is cool and sharp after the stuffiness of the house. Round the corner, I hear for the first time the dull rumble of traffic on the high street; cars, people, lives being lead in all their precious normality.

In the newsagents, the owner and one of the customers ask after my father and say that they have not seen him for a while; how is his health, how does he manage for company? They know about his illness, but do not dwell on it; they know how serious it is. They say they must get round to see him more, but I know that they won't. One tells me about the people at church who are praying for my father, too. They have candles lit for him in the side chapel and a photograph of him on the notice board with a simple message saying, In our prayers. "He's sorely missed by everyone," she tells me, and while they hope for the best they fear the worst.

I buy a newspaper and I go round to a nearby bar and sit down to read it with a pint. The landlord comes and sits next to me and he too asks after my father. It seems most of the people in our part of town know him.

When he goes I get round to the paper. There are stories of a car bomb in Pakistan, an assassination in the Lebanon, fear of a pandemic in Asia. Somewhere a model has had her breasts enlarged.

I close the newspaper and finish my pint. As I leave, the barman reminds me to say hello to my father and I nod in return. The streets on the way home are empty, poised for the return of school children and those who are out to work. The man is now vacuuming the inside of his car.

As soon as I enter the house, I hear their voices from upstairs. The nurse is still laughing. I go up and, from the landing, I see them through the crack between the door and the frame. I see the nurse's back and his face, watching her. I do not stay there for long. As I move, the floorboard creaks.

He is still sitting up in bed and she is talking to him. She turns to smile as I enter the room and behind her my father nods towards her, picking up the innuendo where he left it. I sit at the foot of the bed opposite her to watch my father talking to the young nurse.

When she gets up to leave, I get up with her. She lays her hand on my father's forehead then pats him on the hand and tells him to be good. I follow her out of the room, telling my father I will be back in a moment. As I go down the stairs behind her I get a feint smell of her perfume; I watch her bright hands on the old worn banister.

In the kitchen she gets straight to her question.

"Did you go?"

"I couldn't."

"Oh, Col." She looks sad rather than angry. It is the look I remember my mother having when she tried to tell me off. "You have to do it at some point."

"I can't."

"You need to talk it through with your father before you do anything."

"I know."

After I left the bar, I had an appointment to see my father's doctor, arranged through the hospital; I was to set up an examination for my father in advance of planning for him to go into care. But, when I got to the clinic and faced the receptionist, once again I had lied and told her I could not make the appointment; something important had come up. She looked at me over her glasses as she scored my name out on the list and handed me another appointment card.

"I just can't do it," I tell the nurse again. "Not yet."

"Why not?"

"He never put my mother in to care."

"Do you want me to set something up?"

"Possibly."

"We all deserve a break, you know?"

"I'll ring you."

"Make sure you do. This is not good for either of you."

I see her to the door and she smiles once more as she leaves. As soon as the door clicks shut the banging from upstairs starts again. I go up and sit on his bed, halfway along.

As I lower myself on to the mattress I feel the aging springs sag weakly. My father is lying on his back with his mouth slightly open and his arms straight down by his side on top of the eiderdown. The feint scent of the nurse's perfume lingers in the room briefly making it smell alive.

"What were you talking about?" he asks.

"Nothing."

"You were a long time talking about nothing."

"It was nothing."

"This house needs a woman."

"Look, we both miss mum, you know. What else do you want?"

He is silent again. I shouldn't have said that. It always makes him go quiet. It is the thought he will never express, but which sits, unspoken, in the silences between everything we say.

I look at him lying in the bed, thinking that there must come a point when we cross a threshold and accept that we want someone to die and that they too want it. But that time is not yet.

I too have been ill in that bed.

It started as a cold but got much worse until I spent several days in a dream-world brought on by the fever. Just before it started, my father carried me out of my room and through to their bed. On the first day, the doctor took my temperature and as he read the scale on the glass tube, he turned and looked at my mother. She wiped her hands on her apron and held her palm against my forehead. After that, the fever began to take over and I spent the next days moving between reality and images and dreams. And all through it she sat by my side and gave me drinks; and food too, when she thought I could swallow it. Between these times she descended into a motionless silence, at that level where there was nothing but my pathetic little needs. She sat there day and night, trying to sleep in the chair, at a point where the only thing that existed for her was me.

When I began to recover she allowed herself to sleep in my bed, but she still came when I called in the night and spent the days sitting by me. Only when I was back in my own bed many days later did she relent and leave me alone for any time. My father was banished to sleep in the tiny spare-room amongst the unused suitcases and boxes.

When I was recovering from being ill, but was still allowed to sleep in their bed, my father came in to see me at the end of each day after he finished work. From lunch-time I began to look forward to his arrival. The music on the radio changed, preparing for the early evening audience. The DJ's took on a more serious tone and news came more frequently. Eventually, as the light outside began to fade, I would become excited about my father's return. Each day he brought me a small present; a comic or some sweets. But I was keenest just to see him and eager for him to read to me. He started to read Treasure Island and, when he was at work, I carried on reading, so that each night he would ask:

"Right, Big Man, where are we up to?"

And I would explain what had happened in the book since he last read to me. Then later, when it was nearly time for me to go to sleep, he would pick up from that point. He read out the voices and tried to put on accents. But as I tired, his voice would become calmer and softer so that, as I gradually fell asleep, the line between the story and my sleep became blurred and intangible.

On the day we finished Treasure Island I was beginning to fall asleep as he came to the end. He lay the book on my chest and, crossing my arms over it, he picked me up. I clutched the book like a bible. Then he carried me back into my room; I was only just aware of that last gentle journey as he laid me in my own bed. Slipping between the cool covers, I remember feeling like I was coming home.

"Night, Big Man," he said, laying his hand on mine before moving away and pulling the door shut.

I look down at my father again and assume that he is asleep. I think about touching his outstretched arm, but instead my hand hovers momentarily before I withdraw it. I leave him and go back to the kitchen. Outside it is now dark. I am just filling the kettle when, from upstairs, comes the banging on the floor. At the foot of the stairs, I shout up that I will be there soon and, to my surprise, the noise stops. There is then a quietness on the house that is always there, behind his banging and our arguments. Our own tip-toeing, silence.

And I think that it is here in this house, and a million places like it, that the real stories of the world unfold; step by step, only vaguely sensing what the future might look like. This is no adventure. There is no treasure at the end.

If he does go into care, I will need to think about what happens to the house; it is tired and needs new life in it. I will have to sell it to pay for whatever he needs. But, when that happens, where they now remain shut, doors and windows will be opened wide to let the air sweep through the house. A new family, perhaps with children of their own, will move in and their shouts and laughter will course through the house.

So, when the time comes, all the boxes and rubbish and clutter of our lives will need clearing out. The broken furniture, the chipped ornaments, the faded curtains, the peeling wallpaper. Those awful pictures in the sitting room.

They will all need to go.

That cooker, this table, these chairs.

Our bed.

Country Park

Nick is ill. His teacher rings me at lunchtime. As she speaks to me down the phone, she occasionally addresses him in the background. I can hear his thin voice as he answers her questions and he sounds close to tears. I need to go to him.

"Tell him I'm coming," I say.

"He'll be alright for a while."

"No, tell him I'm coming."

"Your mother's coming to get you." The teacher's voice becomes distant as she turns away to speak to him.

"Tell him I'm leaving right now. Please tell him that."

I leave work to catch the two buses across town. When I arrive at the school, he is in the sick room, sitting on the hard bed with his feet dangling over the edge. I stand in front of him and he buries his small head in my stomach and cries as I rest my hands on his hair and pull him close to me.

"Come on, let's go home," I say eventually.

"Please."

"I'll get your bag."

On the bus, he rests his head on my shoulder. At home I put him on the couch, where he sleeps and as I stroke his hair I think how much he looks like his dad.

Before we were married, his father came into the flat we shared one day with some coach tickets and just announced, "We're going to Blackpool. It's all organised," and so we went. We'd never been on a coach trip before; we got to the sea very rarely.

On the coach he rested his head against me while I stroked his hair. When we arrived we went straight to the funfair, where he pulled me onto the roller coaster; I thought I'd be sick as it plunged and weaved into the steepest curves, but he put his arm around me and instead I laughed and screamed. He let go of me for a while, and raised both of his arms and shouted while we pitched and wheeled. I kept screaming and laughing until the small carriages pulled to a stop and we got out. My legs buckled as I stepped out and he reached out to hold onto me. He held me tightly before kissing me.

"You alright?" he asked

"I'll be fine."

"Sure?"

"Sure," and he kissed me again.

We walked along the edge of the sea where the small waves pushed sheets of bright surf up the beach. I took off my shoes and socks to walk in the water, its cold sharpness numbing my feet. Later we got our photographs taken in a booth and before we caught the coach back we walked to the end of the pier to look back on the people still crowding onto the beach and filling the sea's margins.

On the way home, the coach stopped in the country at a pub with a large room at the rear. Most people off the coach went in for something to eat, but the building backed onto a canal so we went for a walk. A short way along the towpath we climbed over a gate and lay down behind a hedge facing the early evening sunshine. He put down his leather jacket for me to lie on and I lay against his chest with my eyes closed, the gentle heat from the sun warming my face.

As we lay by the river, I heard the birds singing behind and above me. Their noise filled all the air around us. I felt myself drifting into sleep. At first I was not alive to him running his mouth down the side of my face to my neck, kissing my temple, my earlobe, the top of my shoulder. At each place, he paused briefly before he moved finally to the nape of my neck. He then pulled the edge of my summer dress away to kiss me lower. He nuzzled my throat and then my chest between my breasts.

"Should we?" I asked.

"It's alright."

"What if someone hears?"

"It'll be fine."

I said no more as he continued kissing me. He unbuttoned the front of my dress so that he could kiss my breasts, and then, as he lifted the hem of my dress, I moved slightly so that he could pull the back of it up to my waist. He swore quietly as he wrestled with his own belt, and he groaned softly as he struggled to pull his trousers down. But then, behind the hedge, next to the canal, we made love quietly, just in case some of our coach-party passed on the tow path. When we finished, the urgency and fumbling and the silence made us laugh. We lay back and laughed until the nervousness subsided. Then around us, through the peace, the noise of the birds returned. And beyond the birds, there was the canal and further still were the fields and all the villages which dozed in the late evening sunlight.

As we went back into the bar, one of the older women on our coach said, "Been for a nice walk?"

"Yes." I replied. Before we sat down to join them, I excused myself, and headed for the toilets, mouthing, "It's running down my leg."

Then we sat for the rest of the evening next to each other talking to these people that we had never met, buying round after round of drinks until it was time to get back on the coach.

Later that week, he bought a map of where we'd visited and put a big red mark on it where we made love, with the words "Here be dragons." Nine months later Nick made his appearance. Five years after that, his dad ran off.

Nick settles on the couch so I go next door. There, sitting on my neighbour's front steps while getting the last of the light, I realise I am tired and my eyes begin to droop. Vicky brings a cup of coffee and sits down next to me. Her hair, usually tied up on her head, comes loose, a strand of it falling over her face. I notice her long ear-rings, heavy with semi-precious stones.

"Your ear-rings are nice." I say

"Thanks. They were a present."

I am lucky to have her next door. I ask her if she can look after Nick tomorrow and as usual she says it's no bother. I kiss her and tell her she's a love then we sit there, on her front door-step, and drink our coffee. Nick is still at my house, asleep on the couch and her three are playing upstairs.

At the end of her short front-yard, the slow rumble of rush hour traffic is growing more regular as it tumbles over the speed humps, like trains passing over a level crossing.

Next morning, I drop Nick round at Vicky's. He's sleepy and warm, bundled up in his duvet. I want to stay with him, but must go to work as I owe them the hours.

"Stay as late as you want," she says.

"Thanks."

"Stop thanking me."

I work late and make up the time. My supervisor is good to me, I suppose, but sometimes it is hard to tell which way it will go with her; it could go either way. Most things could go either way.

I miss the seven o'clock bus and ring Vicky. She says not to panic; it's all fine. Everyone is OK. They'll be fed and ready for bed when I get back. I go to the waiting room where I find a seat by the large glass window and look around the room. The strip light hums, some of the red plastic seats are missing and the frames for posters are all empty. There are stains on the floor where people have spilled canned drinks.

There is a small revolving rack of information leaflets in the corner of the room. Out of boredom, I pick a few out and I read them as I wait for the bus. One is for a country park somewhere outside the city, with pictures of swans, a fox, and some children with nets, pond dipping at the edge of a lake. I take it with me to read on the bus.

I go straight to Vicky's when I get back. Her front room is full of washing waiting to be ironed. In a corner of the room, the television is on, a semi-circle of children on the floor around it. I look for Nick, but he is not here and as I turn to Vicky, she anticipates my question.

"He's upstairs. He's fine."

And I sit down and start to cry. She moves the washing and sits next to me, and puts her arm around me.

"I'm sorry," I say.

"Don't be."

"It's just hard at the moment."

"I know...coffee?"

"Please. I'm sorry. Is he really alright?"

One of the children turns around to look at us, so we get up and leave the room. I go and sit on her front step, and she joins me with the coffees. The few shrubs and plants that she has are in full leaf. The large tree on the road-side blocks out some of the evening sun. The coffee is strong and I feel its effect.

"I spend my life here," she says. "...on this step, watching everyone in the city drive past to and from work."

"I know what you mean."

"I sit and dream, and someday I'll end up saying *that was my life*."

"Don't" I say. "We should do something."

"Such as?"

"When Nick's better, do you fancy a trip somewhere?"

"Like where?" she says.

"Don't know. The seaside...the country? It's just that I never do anything anymore. I never go anywhere."

"Sounds good."

And then we sit in silence as the coffee helps me to get my composure back before I go and see Nick. In the room, I perch on the side of the bed as he sits up. I show him the leaflet about the country park and tell him we will go there when he gets better. I point to the pictures of the animals and enthuse about the possibility of seeing foxes and badgers to cheer him up.

At the weekend, I tidy the house and then try to do some work outside. But Vicky and her husband come round with a bottle of cheap white wine and we sit in my yard and drink it as the children run around us. Nick is back to normal now.

"Do you fancy next weekend?" I say.

"How do you mean?" says Vicky.

"For the trip. To the country park."

"You're keen."

"I need to get on...*do* something."

I can tell that she's forgotten. I don't press it, so we sit there and drink the wine. Her husband holds the drink up to the light and swills it around the glass. He tips it slightly and watches the sun glint off the liquid's surface. It is a yellow, slightly green colour. The top edge of the wine is shining diamond bright in the sun. Vicky and I watch him again swill it around the glass, hold it to his nose and smell it. Then, he finally takes a drink.

"What the hell are you doing?" asks Vicky, laughing then looking at me.

"Savouring the wine. I think I'll become an expert." he says, smiling at her.

I keep Nick off for a couple more days. On the Wednesday he stays in the house on his own and on Thursday he goes back to school. Sitting on Vicky's doorstep, that evening I ask her again about the trip, but she tells me she can't do it this weekend. She'd forgotten that she had to visit relatives. So, in my head I plan to make the trip the following weekend. At work I check bus timetables on the web, and I begin to get excited about going. But Nick comes back from school and tells me he thinks there's something on and produces a letter. The note from the head teacher reminds us about the school show that all the children are involved with. Nick's been practicing for weeks.

"Shit. I'd forgotten," I say.

"I only just got the letter." says Nick.

"That's alright."

"I was off. It's not my fault."

"I said it's alright." I try not to make my voice sound edgy.

On Saturday evening, therefore, we catch the bus to the school. From the bus stop we walk the short distance to the school; the route that Nick does every day of his school life. Each corner, each place will be part of his memory. Then, over the years, this bit of his life will shrink until it is just a few remembered things. Like meeting his friends, like worrying before exams. Or like a ride on a roller coaster and kissing in a photo booth, then all that is left will be the small bright moments and he too will end up saying *that was my life.*

More people are arriving at school. When we reach the gates there are small clusters of parents and children, some I recognise. Nick shouts to his friends and I pass the time with some of the parents. One asks me if Nick's better.

"I think so," I say

"Till the next time."

"Yes. Till the next time," and I laugh a small laugh.

The school show is a musical. They sing pop tunes, but with new words. They make fun of the teachers or the school. Nick has to sing a song from "Grease". He has the part of a gang member with his hair slicked back and a black jacket that's too big for him. I think again how much he looks like his dad. It's a fact that will always be there. My friends avoid saying it, but it's what they think. It's what I think, too.

At the end of the show, Nick doesn't take his makeup off. He's proud of his performance and I hug him and say well done. As we stand at the bus stop, he sings the song and starts to skip around, dancing to the tunes in his head, but he stops when other people arrive. He keeps the leather jacket on, with the collar turned up.

In Vicky's kitchen that weekend I say:

"I am going this Saturday...whatever happens."

"Where?"

"The country park."

"Decisive or what, Sal?"

"No question. Come hell or high water."

"I can't make it. I'm on late shift. Sorry."

"No matter. I'll take yours."

"What? All of them?"

"Sure. Why not?" I say.

I arrange to take her three children along with Nick.

During the week I assemble as much information as I can. I collect all of the leaflets and timetables and pile them on the edge of our kitchen table. On Thursday, Nick starts coughing and I worry partly for him, but mostly for me. I want to make the trip so badly that I keep him off on Friday, but do not tell Vicky; I just let him stay in bed.

On Saturday morning, Nick is up early and by the time I go into him, he is dressed, has a bag packed and it is sitting at the foot of his bed. I pack spare clothes for him, just in case. After breakfast, we go next door to pick up the other children. Vicky is still in her dressing gown.

"It's alright for some," I say.

"It was your idea."

Her children come banging downstairs and run into the kitchen. The children start to shout. Vicky's youngest is excited, but not sure what about so she just runs around on the spot. I take the buggy, but load it up with the bags.

"Having second thoughts?" asks Vicky.

I shake my head.

"What are you going to do?" I ask.

"Go back to bed before my evening shift."

"Oh yes?"

"To sleep, Sal, that's all. I'm on nights. Remember the rules, no sex on night-shift days." she says.

We sit near the front of the bus and have to change at the depot and get a different one to the other side of the city. It's still only nine o'clock when we get onto the second bus and, as I don't know where we're going, I ask the driver to let me know when we get to the stop. The children all run to the back of the empty bus to sit on the back.

On the long back seat, Nick's showing Vicky's son what he has in his pack. He has his sandwiches, some paper and pencils, some toy soldiers. He also pulls out a pair of binoculars and then a map.

"We can go exploring," he says, "I found this old map."

"Can I have a look," I say, leaning across the seats.

He hands me the map. I open it and in the middle of one of its sections is a big red circle, with the words "Here be dragons." printed next to it. A row of three small photographs of his dad and me fall out onto the floor. I pick them up.

That day at the seaside, between each flash in the photograph booth, his dad and I struck our poses. For the first frame, we pulled faces with our tongues out and our eyes wide open. Then we tried to smile amongst the chaos in the small cubicle. With the third flash, I fell off the small stool as he tried to move me round to sit on his knee. Finally, we kissed, our eyes closed oblivious to the last flash. We carried on kissing after the pictures had all been taken and it was only when there was a cough from outside the cubicle that we stopped. He took his hand away from the top of my thigh and I straightened my dress. When we stepped out of the cubicle there was an old woman waiting to go in. We hurried away when our photographs emerged. He waved them in the air to dry them, before folding them to put them into his pocket.

On the coach, on the way back from the pub, we sat on the back seat. We both fell asleep from the beer and only woke when we got back to the coach station. Sleepily, we walked home through the streets that were quiet and still, him looking so good in his leather jacket with the collar turned up, and me in my new dress. That evening, I cut off the picture of us kissing, and put it in my purse.

In the weeks and months that followed the trip, our life was content. We were not consciously happy, but there was a pattern to our life that I knew I would look back on one day and think "I was happy then". Life was precious for a while. And in the remembering of it, I knew it would take on the sheen of happiness. Even now, when I talk it through with Vicky, telling her what we did that day we went to the seaside, that is what she says; "You must have been happy then."

But as our life together unravelled, the changes were subtle at first. I suggested we spend more time together. Another trip to the seaside or back to the canal. Or anywhere just to get away. But we never made it, there was always something in the way.

And then he was gone.

I ask Nick, "Where did you get this map?"

"I found it at home. No-one wants it." He is defensive.

"It's OK. It's not of round here you know?"

"Where is it?"

"Somewhere a long way away."

"I can pretend though, can't I?"

"Of course you can."

I hand him back the map.

"What does 'Here be dragons mean'?" he asks.

"Nothing really."

"Are there?"

"Not anymore," I say.

We travel out of the city along the river, the industrial buildings giving way to the bright new flats offering bright new lives. Gradually these too fade away and we travel along narrowing roads which begin to rise into the hills. I look out of the window; I see a pub, woods, a river. As we pass over a bridge, I look along the river and briefly see the trees and, beyond them, the fields and hills gently nudging in along the waterway. I think maybe I remember somewhere like it... but no, it's not the same.

Instead, I turn to watch Nick going through the contents of his bag with his friend. The map lies on the seat next to him.

After ten more minutes, the bus driver shouts for us to get off. It's our stop. I check the times of the return buses. I have tight hold of the hand of Claire, Vicky's youngest. We are opposite the entrance to the country park. There are no other people around, nor any traffic once the bus has turned a bend out of sight.

We spend the day moving slowly and with little purpose between the different parts of the site. We go to the new visitor centre and watch a short video about the wildlife. Then I suggest we go and look for the foxes we saw in the film. There is a guided tour around the lake which we join and the children are given small trays to try to collect bugs. The park ranger helps us identify the insects and tells us their names. He gives the children badges with the name of the park on them which they pin on as we eat our packed lunches on the picnic tables outside the centre. Vicky's youngest is in the buggy, now fast asleep. After, we walk round the lake again, with Nick and Vicky's son rushing off into the trees, and the other two following them. They play hide and seek, and chase each other while Claire and Sophie collects sticks and we have a long talk about how many she can take home.

Around tea-time, the park empties of people; as if someone has pulled a plug out somewhere. It's time for people to head home and there is, for a while, a stream of cars leaving the car park.

There's an hour to the bus. It will be at least another hour after that before we get home. The visitor centre is locking up, but we just get in to buy a last ice cream and we eat them outside.

The day has gone well; it could have gone either way. I am happy we came.

We walk one last time through the park to the play area where the boys run off to ride on the zip-line, but Vicky's middle-daughter Sophie just stays near me. She plays in the small wooden house, collecting stems of grass and pretending it's food. She asks me to drink an imaginary cup of tea.

"I prefer coffee." I say, so she goes back to the wooden house to make me a pretend cup of coffee.

I sit on a bench next to Claire, who is asleep again in the buggy. There is a coolness in the air now although the sun has come out from under a low bank of cloud and it is hovering near the horizon. There are small strands of mist beginning to gather on the surface of the lake and there is a feint smell of smoke too. I look around and in the clump of trees on the other side I see a thin plume rising in a perfectly straight line. A group of ducks glides across the surface of the lake. They leave a small series of ripples spreading, vague as a shadow, across the still water. I close my eyes against the sun and breathe in the distant smoky scent, imagining layer upon layer of this calm.

I am not sure whether I fall asleep, or just lose attention, but I suddenly hear one of Vicky's children scream. I open my eyes and look across the play area. Sophie is near the swings, lying on the ground with Nick standing over her. The swing is still moving. A small bruise is beginning to form on her forehead. Nick is standing totally still, staring at her and screaming.

"I didn't see her. I didn't see her. I didn't see her."

I am by their side in seconds. I tell Nick it's alright, it was an accident. I calm him down and then I pick up the girl.

"I didn't see her."

"It's alright." I say. "It's alright," and I stroke his hair while I cuddle the girl.

She's not badly hurt. She cries for a short while and then her sobs grow quieter as we sit on the ground. She relaxes as the bruise gathers the colour of blackberries on her brow. Then she falls asleep, her small taught body going limp. Nick and Vicky's son return to the swing.

And in my arms, Sophie sleeps, all the possibilities of her own precious life once more put on hold until she awakens.

Archaeology

Each day, at the head of the valley, they burned the cattle to dispose of the carcasses. The bitter smell was carried on drifts of smoke down the hill and was everywhere. It got into our clothes, into our hair. It reached, I am sure, the village down the valley where it would seep into the memory of the young children. I stood and watched with my father from the gate that leads from our farm to the site being used for burning. It was as far as we were allowed to go. Beyond there, only Ministry officials who were supervising were allowed to pass. Our cattle had already been shot and burned. They caught the disease early on. We were watching other people's cattle being burned now.

"There's nothing left to do," he said.

"We'll get the compensation".

"That's not it." he said. And we turned to retrace our steps, back towards the farm, spending several minutes scrubbing the strong disinfectant into our protective footwear. The liquid was thick and yellow. Even through the clothing, we could feel our skin prickle and our eyes water. As my father scrubbed, I looked up and across the hills. There was still some snow on the distant fell-tops.

In the kitchen, my mother had prepared lunch. We ate

in silence, as we usually did then. There was not much to do on the farm with the cattle gone and the disease still around. There was little to be said. When father spoke, he kept telling us he would buy some more stock when the burning was over. I once asked him why and he simply answered, "Because."

The kitchen was always the warmest room in the house. It continued to smell of animals; still smelled of a working farm. The two dogs came and went as normal although we could not let them out across the fields. Our days were spent sitting in the thin light of the kitchen. I would read the newspapers and the farming magazines, my finger running down the pages as I read. If the door opened, the smell of burning came back into the room from off the hill.

We mostly spoke to our neighbours on the telephone, following the spread of the disease through them and the press. My mother's habit was to cut out the important articles and keep them.

I was young when I first discovered her old cuttings. My parents were out and I was looking for hidden Christmas presents. They'd gone to the village for a dance, leaving me with my elder brother. It was him who suggested we look for the presents. He said that they wouldn't be back for hours. I went into their bedroom where I didn't find any presents, but in their dark wardrobe I found old newspaper articles. They were in a box with other papers – tickets for dances, photographs of them when they were younger. There were layers of things she'd kept. Those at the bottom of the box were from a time before my brother and I were even born. I found cinema tickets from the days when the village hall showed films. There were two tickets with the name of the film hand-written on the plain numbered pieces of paper. In the box, I also found articles that told of the last outbreak of Foot and Mouth. There was a picture of the vans and lorries parked outside the village. Another showed three or four men standing staring at the camera. They were wearing short white coats over their normal clothes. A policeman was close by. These pictures had intrigued me back then. I spent a long time looking at them. I thought about how, in the middle of it all, they'd gone to see a film in the village hall. The tickets nestled snugly between the two photographs and the articles.

My brother shouted from the spare room that he'd found the presents, so I tidied up the box, and pushed it to the back of the drawer where I'd found it. The drawers smelled of my parents; of my mother's talcum powder, the smell of my father's jackets and the subtler, older smell of wood.

There was still meagre work to do on the farm. With the beasts gone, we needed to disinfect the buildings. A few months after our cattle had been burned I started on the barns. I returned one evening from cleaning them, ready for the eventual return of the cattle. My mother was cutting out an article at the kitchen table. I asked her what it was about. She told me to wait until she had finished and that I could read it then. But, I was eager to leave, and before she finished I set off for the village for a drink with my friends. There, in the pub, we fell into the routine of drink. The talk was of the disease, who's farm had it, and how far it had spread. Over a game of pool one of my friends asked.

"How's your brother?"

"OK. Don't hear from him much."

"Has he got a woman?" my friend asked.

"Not that I know of."

"He got out at the right time."

"Too right." I said, as I hammered in the black, the frustration of months released momentarily.

From the back bar, I could hear the sound of the juke-box. As I racked-up the balls again and lined-up behind the cue-ball, I knew who was in the bar by the music that had been selected. I knew the sequence the tunes would follow.

What routine there was without the cattle numbed us all. At supper one evening, my mother produced the box of cuttings, tickets and articles that normally stayed in their room at the back of the wardrobe drawer.

"You might be interested in this" she said. "It'll give you something to do for a while". I didn't want to tell her I had seen much of it when I was younger. I already knew most of its contents. In the tense, illicit silence of their room years ago, I used to read the articles that my mother had cut out; the articles from the local press about the village, those concerning our school, sports days, a catalogue from the village show with my name for coming second in some competition. Reading my name back then had set my heart racing. There were articles about the valley where we lived. There was even one from the national press; a faded Sunday supplement that the country would have read. It had filled me with pride to think that everyone had read about our valley.

But not since my brother left had I been back to the box. His going was a fracture in all our lives. On the day he left, there was mostly silence in the kitchen. My mother had cooked a large full breakfast, trying to joke that it would be the last good meal he would eat for some time. He told them he would write and come back often. His first purchase was going to be a car, he said. The smell of the cooking meat hung deep and rich in the kitchen. There was a clatter of moving crockery and cutlery, but little conversation. About half an hour before my brother left for the bus, my father had got up saying that he needed to go and sort out the cattle. The dogs got up instinctively and went to the door as he rose.

"Can't they wait, this morning?" my brother had asked.

"No", said my father, and he held out his hand to shake my brother's hand.

As their grip slackened, my father turned and picked up his jacket and left.

The box my mother put on the table was still the same one. It was more worn, and full to over-flowing because of all the additional cuttings. The sides of the box were beginning to bend and tear and were held together with sticking tape. The order of the collection was still the same though. There were fewer tickets and programmes on the surface, fewer days away from the farm to relieve the work. On the top of the collection was the article she had been cutting out the previous week. I sat at the kitchen table, looking through the box, careful not to upset the order of things.

I turned up some of the layers that gave me such pleasure when I used to steal into their room. There was a musty smell to these pieces, the paper was brittle and dry. For the first time in many years, I read about the village show, sport's days and about my brother's games for the rugby team. I looked again through the old photographs of the previous outbreak of Foot and Mouth disease. One faded black and white photograph showed uniformed officials delivering a large container of disinfectant to a farm. Another simply showed the signs that were used to warn people off the land. These made more sense to me now.

And, I read the ageing piece from the Sunday press about our valley. The photograph in the article was taken from the hill opposite. You could see our farm and the buildings clustered around the farmhouse. It was taken before the new metal barn was built, long before the burning. The article told the history of where we live. The Romans came, mixing with the local tribes and when they left, it was the Vikings. They landed near here, on the coast where the river valley meets the sea. They spread out through the hills, but when they receded, like the tide going out, they left us their own driftwood. In settlement patterns, in hidden timber beneath the ground, but mostly in the names of places. Like in the name of our village and those up and down the valley as well as in the names of the farms and the individual fields. They came and went. And eventually my father farmed the land.

"Why do you keep these things?" I asked when I had finished digging through the box.

"The past sustains us," she said.

"Do you believe that?"

"It's true for some of us."

"Not for me, I don't think."

"I know that."

On the farm, the burning has stopped and the land covered over. The buildings have been cleared out and cleaned with disinfectant. We are free to come and go as we please.

I drive my father to the local market. We look at some

cattle to replace the ones we lost. The compensation will be through soon and he can start to rebuild his stock. At the market, he casts his eye over all the lots of cattle. He complains that they are a bit thin. He says they are from the south, and too soft for our hills. But he still rubs his hand along their hides and pats them on their thick muscular necks. I return to the room where they serve tea, sitting with my back against the wall in the corner. There, I listen to the radio and watch him through the windows that look out onto the yards. On the way back, he talks about the other farmers, some of whom he has not seen for several months. He tells me how they have done over the past year. Who is still farming, who is staying in and who is getting out.

As we get back into the house, he takes out the catalogue from the market, and tosses it onto the kitchen table.

"Put that in your collection," he says to my mother. "First auction for nearly a year."

And she picks it up and sets it to one side to put into the top of the box when she goes to bed that evening.

Over supper, I say, "I've been thinking..."

"What have I told you about thinking?" he says, interrupting, not wanting me to get to the end of the sentence. As I speak, I stare down at the table, moving my hand across its surface, smooth with years of use. I spin the fork round mechanically. I know they are watching me.

"I've been thinking. I won't be following you onto the farm."

The kettle boils, and my mother jumps up, startled, to take it off the hob. She stands it on the draining board and remains standing, facing the range moving the dishes and the pans around.

"As you will," says my father eventually.

"What will you do?" asks my mother turning round from the range.

"I'm going to visit our James."

And, there is no more to be said.

My father farms this land and I will not.

I wait for the cattle to return before I go. I help my father get them into the clean sheds. He slaps each one on its side as it passes, and he looks over the shed gate at them for a while after he has penned them all in. It is nearly a year since there were cattle here.

A week later, I leave with a hand shake from my father and a brief hug from my mother.

I drive down the valley towards the main road. It is growing dark, and I switch on the headlights. There is snow, again, on the high fells. At first, I pass only isolated farms with their inside lights switched on. Further down the valley, I start to pass through the villages. My headlights arc across the village name-plates, each one picked out in the beams of light. As I leave each village, I look in my rear-view mirror to look at the sign. I descend the valley, towards the main road leading south. The road is easier now and I can pick up a bit of speed, so I drive more quickly. And behind me, the names of the villages unfurl like pages of a book.

Risen

The bus climbs the steep road from the coast, raising a ribbon of dust which drifts away behind us across the mountain and down the slopes. On our right, the hill falls away as a series of cliffs and ridges. Through the dust and the heat-haze, across the plain, I can make out the slight changes of colour where the Mediterranean and the sky meet.

I lean against the window to cool my head; take a sip from my bottle of water. Ahead of us an old lorry, loaded down with what looks like sugar cane, moves slower and slower until it almost comes to a stop. Our driver moves down through the gears until eventually the lorry and the bus both come to a halt on the empty road. We sit and wait. Beneath me, around me the dull thrum of the engine reverberates. The old bus shudders with each turn of the motor. The engine slows like a toy winding down until the it stalls.

I breathe the hot air and watch a bird rise in a series of short bursts up into the deep blue sky. I watch it for as long as I can until my eyes hurt from staring into the brightness. Then I close my eyes and wait in the stillness and the silence. And across the years, mother, I hear your breathing. It is there in my own breath. In the rhythm of my heart beats. Slow and relentless.

I used to hear you climbing the stairs. Your weight made that step, the one near the top, release its small cry. Out on the landing, in the darkness, you stood still. Your breathing was heavy from climbing the stairs. You were always angry, it seemed.

"Are you asleep, Susan?" you said.

Then you waited.

"I hope you're asleep."

You waited again.

"It's very *very* late."

You stood outside my room making your small noises; the breathing, the swaying as you shifted your weight. I waited until you went down the stairs. Three steps, then the creaking stair and eight more before you reached downstairs. You opened the sitting room door and briefly the sound of the television escaped around the house. The door closed and strangled the noise. The door clicked shut. Then there was the quiet again and the darkness. You sitting alone with your drink and your loneliness watching the television, always angry with me. Me in my bed in the dark.

A noise from outside the bus makes me open my eyes and I look to see what is happening. Our driver is leaning out of his window and shouting to the lorry driver who shouts something back. The truck eventually moves off and pulls over to the side of the road. The bus-driver starts the engine again and we move slowly up the hill and, as we pass the lorry, I look at its old driver. He is climbing down from the cab. He waves his arm dismissively at the bus. A young boy, maybe his grandson, sits in the passenger's seat smiling at the old man.

The bus stops in a municipal square three hours after we

set off from the seaport and my hotel. The handful of people who get off with me soon vanish into the mesh of small streets leading off the Plaza. They have real families to go to. Cool kitchens, small courtyards or precious corners in which to let the heat fade away. The women in black clothes scurry away with their bags of shopping leaving me alone in the square; Plaza de la Republica. The sun works into the angles of the white walls and casts stark shadows across them and the streets. Blinds are pulled down over the windows and over the dark wrought iron grids around each frame. The bus pulls away to reveal a café. It is the only open building in the square. Inside, five men are drinking in the shade, sitting on high stools at the long bar watching the television. Awnings cover a few empty tables outside on the pavement. The clipped plain trees rustle as I walk across the square and sit at one of the outside tables. I take out my book to read.

I was so scared in the darkness of my room, mother, feeling your moods creeping up the stairs. I used to pull the covers over my head if I wanted to read. They smelled of washing powder. Beneath the covers I heard my heart beating faster; felt it against my nightdress. When my heart beats hard I still know the fear of you switching out my light with you outside muttering at me.

On Saturday or Sunday mornings I hid. I made a den under my bed, alone. I pulled the sheets over the side of the bed and cleared out the pieces of paper and books that had fallen down the side; books that I left on my bed when I fell asleep. You kept cases and boxes under my bed. I moved them too. It was my den. The neat little world that made me feel safe. If I moved all of the suitcases and boxes so that they were half under and half out of the bed, I could fit behind them. In the musty quietness, I lay under the bed with the springs only a few centimetres from my face. Hiding. Then I rolled onto my side to read my books.

My favourite book was the one my Auntie bought from a jumble sale. One page listed the tallest buildings in the world. The tallest building in Britain was so small in comparison to the others. I knew then that one day I would leave you and go to see the world's tallest buildings. One day I would see the world's most beautiful places. My book told me Madrid was the highest capital city in Europe and also the hottest. Paris looked the prettiest.

I kept this with my other books on my bedside table. The largest book was at the bottom. Then the small tidy pile went up in descending order of size. Until at the top was the smallest book, and on top of that, a postcard from my Auntie. But whenever I left the room, you always came in and put things away. You tidied the bed, and moved my books back into the bookcase. You destroyed my small world. You manipulated things into the way you wanted them.

The men in the bar watch me as I settle myself down, then turn to look at the television once again. My guide to Spain tells me about the village "The town, surrounded by hills covered in vines and olives, is a small gem. It has the remains of a Moorish castle, later altered in the 14th Century during the reconquest of the South of Spain by the Christians. There are three churches of interest; San Augustin, San Sebastian and, most spectacular of all perched on the rocky outcrop at the top of the hill on which the village is built, Santa Maria de Jesus...As few tourists get this far from the coast, there is little in the way of food or cafes, but one or two bars provide simple tapas..." I look up from the book and follow the rise of the streets and the hill from where I am sitting. It is a wall of dazzling white, broken only by the deep red of the pantile roofs, but at the top of the hill I can just make out the tower of Santa Maria de Jesus.

The men are in a line along the counter, the smoke from their cigarettes drifting up as they stare, quite still, at the game show on the screen. Eventually, when the adverts start, the bartender comes out to serve me. I order a coffee. He brings me a large cup and a small bowl of olives and some bread. The olives still have their stalks on. They are moist and glistening. I pick one up and roll it in my fingers.

"Graçia." I say.

"De nada."

I put the smooth green, oily olive into my mouth. The waiter knows that I do not speak Spanish, so takes the exchange no further and returns to the television. I drink the coffee and start to write a card to my Auntie Alice. I always choose one that I know will make her want to visit the place. I know what it is that she likes.

When I have finished writing, I look up. Across the square, a woman walks holding the hands of her children, one on each side. She slips silently into the shadow of a street at the end of the square and she is gone. Then Plaza de la Republica is empty again. The only knot of any slight noise or movement is around this bar. I motion to the bar tender for another coffee. He brings it to the table with another small bowl of olives. He puts a napkin under the bowl to stop it blowing away in the breeze that occasionally moves hot air through the square. I feel the air move against my bare arms and legs.

When Auntie Alice came to visit that weekend, the last I can remember to our house, she held my hand as we walked down the street to the park. When we got to the playground, it was empty; I loved it that way. Someone must have just left, though, because the roundabout was still gently turning. Once through the metal gate, I ran towards it; jumped on and let it carry me round. When my auntie caught up with me, she pushed me faster. I sat in the middle of the roundabout and watched her come and go as I spun. I closed my eyes and the movement began to make me feel sick. I tried not to think about it, trying to put off the time when I knew I would have to stop. Eventually though I shouted out.

"Stop it, Auntie, stop it."

When I stood up from the roundabout, dizzy from going round, I fell over onto the tarmac surface. I lay on the ground holding my knee and crying, the world moving uncontrollably around me. My knee was bleeding onto the ground. There was blood on my dress. She sat me down on a seat and wiped my eyes and face with her handkerchief. Then she wet the white cloth in her mouth and dabbed my cut. When we got home, we were late for lunch and you were angry, mother. You shouted at me and sent me to my room for dirtying my dress. Auntie Alice said it was her fault, but you did not listen to her. You said that I was old enough to think for myself. From my room I could hear you shouting at her.

"She has to learn."

"You're too hard on her. You're all she has."

"And who did I have? Answer me that. Who did I have?"

When Alice came up to say goodbye she said she was sorry for getting me into trouble. After that, I cannot remember her coming to our house again. She sent me birthday cards and Christmas presents, but she stayed away until I was nearly sixteen. It took that long for her to heal the hurt you caused her, mother. I loved being with my Auntie Alice; she knew what I liked and she played with me. But all that was spoiled.

The bartender puts his hand on my shoulder. Not a rough touch or even a threatening touch, but I recoil.

"Excuse Signora."

"Si," I say

"Una mas?" he asks pointing to the coffee cup.

"No graçias. La quanta, por favour."

"Ah, si. *The bill.*" and he laughs.

The men watch me again as I stand up to leave. The television still has the game show on with its canned laughter and grinning host. The bartender returns and slips the bill under the olive bowl. He then goes back to his place at the bar, watching the television. I leave the money without waiting for change. He looks up at the screen and he shouts something at one of the contestants. More music, more laughter. I push back the chair. This attracts their attention as it scrapes along the stone floor; they turn to look, then turn back to the programme.

I move off into the shadow cast by the large church, out of the sun into the cool dark. The nameplates for the roads are set high on the walls of the houses; ceramic tiles of deep blue. I am on Via d'el Santa Carmen. The others too are religious or political names. Santa Maria, la Constitution, la Conception. Santa Carmen is deserted.

It rises steeply from the main square. I pass closed, grilled windows, a moped leaning against a wall. In one window, between the shutters and the iron grill, a cat sits amongst the potted geraniums. I look in my rucksack for my camera, take a photograph and watch the cat for a while. When I move off, it too chooses this moment to slide between the bars and walk off. The street opens out onto another square, much smaller though than Republica. Plaza de San Sebastian. One side of the square is dominated by the massive white façade of a church. A small ceramic plaque explains " San Sebastian. Eglis d'el XVII Siecle." White, plain and monolithic, its top half and small bell tower are shining in the light above me.

I push open the big wooden door to the church and step into the cool semi-dark. There are no lights. Behind me, the door swings slowly and closes with an echoing click. At the top of the walls, high windows let in some of the afternoon sun from outside. I walk a few paces until I am aligned with the centre of the nave at the end of which is the alter and, behind that, the large wooden cross. I look for a moment at the cross and the figure. The goldleaf on Jesus' halo reflects some of the light from above, the sunlight also picking out the dust in the air. I walk around the edge of the church. There is a feint smell of incense. I follow the fourteen Stations of the Cross around the walls. I know nothing about them, but I translate some of the words from the adjacent plaques. Each one is exquisitely carved in wood, with the sculptor's name in the bottom right-hand corner. I stop at the sixth station; the one which depicts Veronica wiping the agonised face of Jesus. I look carefully at the detail; the Roman guards standing by as the woman helps him rise to go on with the journey up the hill.

It is truly beautiful and yet it is here, in this small church near the top of its own hill in a remote village with hardly anyone ever seeing it. I realise I have had to wait so long to be able to appreciate small wonders like this. To be alive to seeing a beauty in things. Perhaps at long last I could now enjoy the world's tallest buildings; the world's most beautiful places. The world is not as miserable as you made it out to be, mother.

I sit down at the back of the church to rest and to look at some of the other carvings. I take out my bottle of water and start to take a sip, but then stop. I think, perhaps, it is not appropriate to drink here. I feel the cool air on my bare arms and legs. I feel the goose-flesh creep over my body in the slight draught.

You would not approve of my sleeveless T-shirt and short skirt, mother, or my bare legs and my bright crimson toenails showing through the sandals I bought for the trip. When I came home from school, you always told me how common I looked in my short school skirt. When I started to go out on Saturday nights you would tell me I looked cheap. You went into my room once, and took out of my wardrobe all of the clothes that you considered to be too short or too tight or not to your liking. Clothes I had bought with my own money. You put them on the bed and pointed at them as you shouted at me.

"Where do you go wearing things like that? What are you thinking of? What kind of boys do you meet, and what must they think of you, sniffing round you like that?"

I remember your whole speech. I heard it often enough. Each time, the rage in me would render me speechless and I turned red with frustration. That was something you mistook for embarrassment. But when you had gone, I could only cry with anger. When I did bring boys home, you shamed me in front of them. When I was seventeen, I brought home a boy that I really liked. You shouted at him too; told him and me what you thought about us.

"He's only after one thing," you said after he had left.

"He's not like that."

"They're all like it."

"I don't believe that."

"I *know*. That's why *you're* here. Remember?"

He never spoke to me again and he and his friends avoided me. Around that time, mother, I started to realise that our worlds were moving so far apart that they would never coincide again. I began to see that I was the burden that you carried, our relationship descending into a final silence. You had told me that I was old enough to have the light out, then not old enough to decide what to wear or what my friends should be like. You told me your views on my jobs, my flats and the man I started to live with. And when my relationships failed you seemed pleased.

"At least you'll not be left alone to bring up a child."

"It doesn't have to be like that."

"That's how it ends up. You have their child and they run away. Always, always, always."

All I ever wanted was for you to help me on my way. I wanted you to say other things. That's all. But all I can hear are your steps on the stairs, the one near the top letting out a small, muffled cry when you leave. And then the door to the living room opening, briefly letting out the noise of the television before closing on your angry silence.

I leave the church and continue up the hill. From the church of San Sebastian, I take another narrow street. The surface of the road is set with cobbles and patterned slabs. It is barely wide enough for a car to pass along it, but a few mopeds still lean against the walls of the houses and everywhere there are flowers and plants. Even in the shade of the street, they are abundant and growing strongly. I try to look through the shuttered windows as I pass, but rarely see anything in the gloom of the rooms into which I peer. I do, though, manage to see into one small courtyard. Through a tiled hallway, off which two dark wooden doors are closed, I see an open area. It is tightly flanked by plants; terraces of green framing the small sunlit square. I stand, briefly, looking at it. Its vibrancy draws me, holds me. At its centre is a low stone bowl, set on a pedestal. Water trickles down the edge. From high above the open yard, the sun reflects off the water's surface. The bright, agile flecks of light illuminate the corners of the courtyard, picking out walls, pots and the still leaves.

At the end of the street I turn right and there is a small play area at one end of the next square. At the other end, only another fifty or so metres further up is the church at the top of the hill, Santa Maria de Jesus. I walk through the play area. I try to sit on the swing, but it is too hot. The seat is made of metal. The slide, too, is roasting hot in the full glare of the sun. As I pass, I push the roundabout and watch it revolve on its own. Its metal handles catch the sunlight and it flashes as it turns, the bright splinters of light slowing down until the roundabout finally stops.

Alice is there amongst the flashes, her hand gently helping me at the playground.

After I left home and moved away she would call me at work. She kept in touch. All through the years when I went to college and when I got my job, she acted as our go between.

We met up before I came on holiday. She offered to buy

me lunch like she always did. She bought two glasses of wine when we arrived at the café and while we drank them waiting for the food, she told me I needed to take a holiday; needed to get away.

"It's not that easy."

"Just do it, for once."

I looked down at my wine. I twirled the glass around by the stem.

"Susan, don't fiddle," she said and she laid her hand on mine.

"It's not that easy," I replied.

I looked up. She looked much older, her skin slack on her face and neck. She asked about work and about relationships. I told her there weren't any, I had lost the heart for it.

"You must never do that," she said. "Never, ever do that..." Even she had joined a bowling club where there were lots of nice old men for her to chase. And she talked about her small new flat overlooking the river. "Very posh. You must come and see it now that I'm in."

As she talked, I arranged the napkins and the cutlery until they were straight and symmetrical, tidily reflecting the lights overhead. And I thought why could you and I not talk simply like this, mother? As Alice spoke, it seemed so easy. I could have just picked up the phone to you and talked. Instead, I sat and brushed the crumbs off the table into the palm of my hand and put them onto my side plate. As I tidied the table, Alice passed me an envelope. I opened it and there was a cheque inside for five hundred pounds.

"This will help. Take it."

"I can't. You can't afford this."

"Take it and just go," she said.

"...but Alice..."

"Just go. Anywhere."

"Is this from her?" I asked, as I held the cheque.

"No. It's from me, but she would give it to you if she had it. She never had any money. Not after....well, she just didn't. You should ring her. She still asks after you."

How could I ring her, I asked? After all she had said. After all the spite and the shouting and the resentment. The way she treated my friends.

"All she prayed was that you didn't end up on the same road as her. She knew no other way to stop you."

"Well it certainly worked," I laughed emptily.

"And he used to hit her....A small, well-respected man who wore a suit and went to work at nine o'clock every day who came home and hit her. Did you know that?"

"And that was my fault?"

"No, no...of course not.....but your mother has been angry and frustrated and poor for most of her life. But she did what she thought was best. She really did."

We stood up to leave and outside the restaurant we parted with a hug. I said as a final thought, "Tell her I might ring." Alice gave me another hug, but said nothing. As we embraced I looked over her shoulder at the people stepping round us in the street, some of them looking back to see what we were doing, perhaps wondering why the woman's eyes were filling up with tears.

I brush the small drop from my cheeks and set off across the square, pushing the roundabout one more time before rising up the hill. I head for the large iron gates in front of the church but before I get there, a group of four women emerges from a small side street and bustle between me and the church. One of them, the eldest, is wearing slippers. They look up towards me only briefly, before hurrying on round the corner of the church out of sight. Just as their voices fade into the silence, I reach the gates of the church of Santa Maria de Jesus. They are locked. Disappointed, I sit to recover my breath on the steps outside the gates.

And you are there with me again, mother. I can still hear you on the stairs. You are outside my room. I can just make out your breathing through the closed door.

Only this time not only do I hear you telling me I am old enough to have the light out, and I should not wear such clothes and I should not go out with those boys, but I also hear, for the first time, a hesitancy in your voice; a wavering, worried inflection that has never been there before. Perhaps I can now see, for the first time it was you, mother, who also needed picking up and helping along the way.

I walk round the side of the church, and emerge onto a small terrace at the back where I lean on a low wall. I am there. There is no where else to go. From here, I can see out over the town. I pick out the roof of San Sebastian and its small bell tower, the small square where I had coffee and the awnings that I sat under. I can see the road which the bus came along flanked by olive trees set rhythmically in the yellow soil, its winding route as it falls down towards the sea where it becomes lost in the haze. The sun is still high in the sky, giving the mist that rises on the coast a pale red edge to it blueness. Hidden in there is the city and my hotel. In my room, in the drawer of the bedside table, are the tickets for the flight home, a few coins, my house keys and my car keys. By the side of my bed, there is a pile of books. They are guide-books, novels, phrase books. The largest, a magazine I bought for the flight, is at the bottom and the rest of them are arranged in descending order of size; a nice tidy pile with the postcard to my mother sitting on the top.

I will post it tomorrow.

A Pure Note

He had a job stacking pallets. It didn't amount to much. It was minimum wage and they weren't allowed to take the damaged tins anymore. They had to pay for them. The rules had changed. His mate, Davey, called the new supervisor "The Wee Twat."

"He's up to something," said Davey.

"How do you mean?"

"He's making money."

"For the Company?"

"Yeah. Sure. I bet he pockets it. The Wee Twat."

He took tins back for his neighbour, Mrs. Rae. They were usually the damaged ones that he got cheap, but when he couldn't get them he paid full price and gave them to her anyway.

"You shouldn't," she said.

"I get them free."

"I can't get to the shops."

"Yes."

"....It's my legs."

"I know."

"Are you sure you get them for free, Son?" she said.

"Sure I'm sure," he said.

At work they were being told to come in earlier and to work harder. The supervisor wandered around the shop floor saying "…..The bottom line is this," and "…the bottom line is that."

"There's a bloody recession on you know," he said. "The bottom line is that we must put more boxes on more pallets so more people can buy our products," he said.

"The bottom line is he's a Wee Twat," said Davey.

It was mostly tinned veg they did. Tomatoes, peas, beans, that sort of thing; setting up orders for small shops. As they loaded the tins on to the pallets to shrink-wrap them, Davey told him that the tomatoes in the tins came from Italy and that they grew in greenhouses as big a factory, plastic warehouses the size of a mountain. That way they could get three or four crops a year and save all the water. The peasants and migrant workers lived in clapped-out wooden shacks next to the greenhouses with their mangy dogs and rusty scooters. And they were paid sod all. Davey knew. He'd been there and seen it.

"And they piss in the water too," said Davey.

"They wouldn't be allowed."

"Don't you believe it, Billy-boy. You're too fucking naïve."

Billy felt cheated by this, he wanted the Mediterranean to be dotted with small white villas and open fields, not run down sheds.

"The tomatoes grow in huge plastic greenhouses," he told Mrs. Rae the next morning when he took round some food.

"Do they?"

"As big as a hill side."

"Nothing's ever quite as it seems, is it? It's good of you to bring these cans."

"It's fine."

"I nearly fell yesterday."

"Did you?"

"And I don't feel so good."

"Are you alright?"

"Slowing but still going, Son."

He left her flat to catch the bus for work; he saw it coming and had to run. On the bus, his chest hurt and he could hardly breathe.

From the window, he looked down on the queues at each stop. The people shuffled impatiently, wanting to push ahead of each other, then as they got on they passed him smelling of old clothes and stale cigarette smoke. At one stop, as the bus moved off a woman who had not reached a seat lurched and fell into him. She apologised and moved further down the bus. Through the smell of the dampness he got a waft of her perfume. Briefly, he imagined her putting it on in the morning; smelling so sweet then running for the bus. It was a beautiful smell. It made him think of sunshine; of summer. He tried to see himself on holiday somewhere. A place he had never been, but where all the holidays of his childhood came together.

"Do you still have dreams?" he asked Mrs. Rae that evening.

"How do you mean?"

"You know, hopes, wishes, things you still want to do. Places you want to visit...that sort of thing."

"All my hopes are in the next room now," she said.

"What about nightmares?"

"I've nothing to fear anymore, Son."

She was still not feeling well, so before he left he told her to ring a doctor.

The following Saturday he went shopping for her. As he came out of the supermarket with the heavy bags, the sun broke out and the wet pavements began to steam in the heat. He bumped past the other shoppers as best he could, but he had to keep stopping because of the number of other people and the bags were cutting in to his hands.

He took a side-street that was quieter than the main road; it would get him back home eventually and was easier to walk along. It was an uneventful street, not one he went down often; there was no reason to. There were a few shops, some weed-filled gap sites, but mostly it was maisonette flats and terraced houses, stacked tight as a pallet. One second hand shop was full of mobile phones, cameras and old guitars. Davey would say that they were all knocked off. The guy would be ringing the stuff, dead cert.

He began to sweat in the heat and he stopped to rest his arms. From behind a door, a dog barked at him. Further down the street he stopped again where, in amongst the terraced houses, he noticed for the first time a plaque on the wall next to one of the doors. "Donulti Violins: repairer and maker of fine instruments." He peered into the gloom of the front room. There was a picture on the wall; a line drawing of a person playing a musical instrument. An empty table was next to the window. The rest of the street was the normal run of anonymous houses with mucky curtains and small, half-ignored front gardens, but this one was quiet and clean.

"An odd place for a violin maker," he said, back in Mrs Rae's flat. She was sitting in her small front room. He watched her start to struggle to get up and offered her his hand.

"They've got to go somewhere," she said, shuffling towards the kitchen.

"But there?"

"There are wonders in unlikely places, Billy."

"I suppose so."

"I'll put the kettle on.....I'm grateful for the food, by the way."

"It's nothing. Have you called the doctor?"

"No."

"Do you want me to do it for you?"

He stood and waited for her to agree from the kitchen, but she said nothing. He heard the sound of the kettle coming to the boil as he looked around the sparse room.

On Monday morning, when he got to work the Supervisor was already laying in to one of the lads.

"The bottom line is, Sunshine, that if you don't pull your fucking finger out, you'll be looking for another job..... we'll all be looking for another job." He walked off without acknowledging Billy.

"What was all that about?" he asked Davey.

"Fuck knows. The Wee Twat. I'll fucking nail him, you'll see."

The rest of the shift ran in silence. When the supervisor was in one of these moods everyone knew it was best to keep out of the way; just get on with it. Billy and Davey were working together on a couple of big orders; catering tins and industrial packs of dried food. Pasta and flour as well as tomatoes, cooking oil. Occasionally, Billy thought about where the food came from, but his image of small farms with animals wandering around was being slowly crushed by Davey.

All this stuff was made in industrial units like theirs. Billy shouldn't believe all that old-family-recipe-stuff on the tins.

It was all so much shite. In fact, Davey had spent a couple of seasons in a canning factory out in East Anglia and it was like being in hell. So many peas and carrots coming through that your eyes felt like they were bleeding. Twelve hours of picking-over the conveyor alongside a whole bunch of people who couldn't speak English and were being paid less than minimum. After work there was nowhere to go except back to the hostel with a carry-out. No wonder people went mad out there; or turned alcoholic. Or both. No. Billy-boy was definitely better off where he was, with or without the Wee Twat. At least he wouldn't go mad. It was the least bad option for guys like them.

In the afternoon Billy ran the pallets to the loading bay ready to go on to the lorries that evening when they came back from the day's run. Davey disappeared off somewhere, but they met up at the last coffee break in the canteen.

"Something will kick-off soon, Billy-boy." He rubbed his hands at the prospect.

"Like what?"

"We'll see."

A couple of days later Davey met him at the gate. The yard was quiet; there were none of the forklifts or blokes scuttling about. The main warehouse door was pulled shut. A security guard was sitting on a small wooden chair next to the side-office door, dozing in the shade of the building out of the sun.

"What's happening?" he asked Davey.

"Come and see what we've got for you, Billy-boy."

Davey led him round the side of the building and in to the rear yard. This was normally buzzing with pallets being moved, deliveries being loaded and the supervisor striding around with his file and clip-board. Today, it was still. In one corner of the yard a group of the lads were in the sun round a big table-affair made up of pallets. They were sitting on plastic chairs from the canteen. Someone had set up a big umbrella.

"Welcome to Costa d'el Davey."

"What's happening?"

"The Wee Twat has done it now. He tried to get one of the young apprentices to lift some boxes on his own. The kid tripped and broke his leg. The factory is taped-off while they investigate."

"It's been coming," said one of the others. He was sitting with his shirt open, feet up on the pallets. His chest was already red. "The bottom line is we're withholding our labour 'till it's sorted." The men laughed.

"Besides. It's a sunny day, so we can pretend we're in Italy. Watching the tomatoes grow," said Davey and he winked at one of the men.

A couple of lorries had already arrived at the gates, but they'd been stopped there. One of the men went over to speak to the drivers, who got on to their mobiles, pacing up and down the side of their trucks.

"Is no-one working then?"

"Not at the moment, Billy-boy. All the women have gone home and us lads are guarding the fort.....so relax."

Davey sat down in one of the chairs, un-buttoned his shirt and lit up.

The supervisor came out to speak to them a few hours later. The men remained slouched in their seats while he told them that the young apprentice was OK; it wasn't a complex break. The Health and Safety Inspector had nearly finished his investigation and when that that was completed they could all go back to work.

Couldn't they?

He looked down at Davey.

"And what about working practices?" asked Davey.

"Meaning?"

"Meaning...what about working practices." Davey stood up. He was not a tall man, but he planted himself in front of the supervisor and started to stare him out. Davey was young, but was always pushing to take charge and the others seemed happy to follow. Billy could imagine Davey as a Sergeant Major, eyeball to eyeball with someone bawling them out.

"It's not safe here," said the guy with the red chest coming to stand next to Davey. "*You're* not safe. I'm worried. I've a wife and kids."

The supervisor looked down his nose at Davey and shook his head.

"That's how it is, is it, Sunshine?" He turned and left them standing in the mid-day glare. Davey stayed perfectly still until the Supervisor disappeared into the factory.

"One nil to us, eh?" said Davey. "What do you reckon?"

On his next trip to the shops for Mrs. Rae, instead of just passing the violin maker's house on the way back, he turned up the short path to the front door and rang the bell. Its remote chime echoed from somewhere deep in the house then died away. For a short while there was no noise from inside and he was quietly relieved. He thought about leaving, but then there was the noise of someone coming towards the door. The feet sounded as if they were crossing bare floorboards, then the steps stopped just behind the door; there was the rattle of a lock and the turn of the handle. The man who opened it was tall, thin and he spoke quietly.

"Can I help you?"

Billy had never thought about what to do beyond ringing the doorbell. The tall man looked at Billy over the top of his spectacles; behind him stretched a cool corridor and at the far end a small kitchen.

"Are you the violin maker?" said Billy.

"Yes."

"I was just seeing if you were in."

"I appear to be, although I am just on my way out," he said.

"I can call back."

"Sundays are good for me."

"I'll call back."

"Was there anything in particular?"

"I'll call back," said Billy.

He turned to go, pausing only to say a quick thanks before he picked up the shopping bags. The small metal gate was stiff and squeaked as he opened it with his foot. Aware how strange this must have seemed to the violin maker, he scuttled off, not sure what else he could say.

"Is that strike of yours still going on, Son?" said Mrs Rowe when he delivered the shopping.

"I don't think it's *my* strike."

"Whose strike is it then?"

"I'm not sure. Davey's I suppose."

"Careful," she said "Do what you think best, but things should feel right for you. They should sound true. Like a bell, I always say. It should give a pure note when you tap it. That way you know it's sound. Same with your strike. The company won't think twice about giving you the sack." She started to stand up, but had to sit back down again, her breaths rattling in her throat, knuckles pale from holding on to the chair arms.

"I'll unpack the bags for you,"

"Thanks, Son."

In the kitchen he opened and closed the doors of the units to find where things went. The soft murmur of the radio started up. He heard Mrs. Rae's voice, as fragile as a reed, trying to follow the tune. He didn't recognise it; it was a classical piece. He hadn't a clue about that.

"Have you ever played an instrument?" he shouted through to Mrs. Rae.

"Never. But I would love to have done."

"My parents never let me," said Billy. "They told me to get a trade. Music was for other people, they said."

"You turned out alright though, didn't you, Son?" She hummed more of the tune. "But I would have loved to have played the piano. It's the only thing I wish I'd done."

He found the cupboard where the packets of dried soup went after several attempts. Other than the small cardboard boxes he put in, there was one damaged can of tomatoes and nothing else.

Early on Sunday he set off to see the violin maker. He went through the park where the mist still clung to the bushes. On the other side of the grass a runner jogged along the path towards the tennis courts, past the old woman who usually hung around the park. She was rolling a cigarette, a can of lager open next to her. It was only nine o'clock.

"I'm sorry I'm so early," he said when the violin maker opened the door.

"No problem." The man's voice was like balm.

"I can come back."

"No. Come through," he said.

They went into his small back room. It was sparsely furnished with only a table, a straight-backed chair and a modest bookcase, packed tightly with books and manuscripts. It was structured, ordered and above all quiet. On every wall there were pictures, etchings and woodcuts of violin players and foreign landscapes. Billy looked at the biggest picture for some time.

"Do you know who that is?" said the violin maker eventually.

"No."

"It's Stradivarius....."

Billy nodded.

"The greatest violin maker of them all?" Billy turned back to the picture. "He worked in Cremona...the Po Valley? Italy?" said the violin maker.

Billy's silence drifted on. "A lot of the food at work comes from Italy," he said to fill the quietness.

The man seemed to take this as a cue.

"In the sixteenth and seventeenth century Italy was at the heart of everything. And for violin makers the Po Valley was the place to be. There were dozens of craftsmen who worked in that area...and they were pretty much all men, as far as we know. I don't know why they chose there," he said. "Perhaps it was because of the wood, perhaps because of the local musicians and music. Perhaps just because someone set-up a workshop and the rest gravitated there. People came from all over the world to learn the trade. It's near Venice, and Venice was the centre of our world in those days. Whatever the reason, once a few craftsmen set up their businesses it took on a momentum of its own and it has remained a centre of craftsmanship ever since." He moved to a watercolour of the Po Valley. "I try to get there at least once every couple of years. To recharge my batteries, so to speak."

And in one unimagined leap, Billy's heart came to rest in a location that he had never seen or heard of. A quiet, calm place that was the distillation of all his childhood holidays and through which ran the thread of craftsmanship; that word that the violin maker used so often...craftsmanship which had passed through centuries and wars and countries to alight here in a street next to his.

The man told him of French influences and German influences. He pointed out the subtle differences in the necks of the instruments, in the fingerboards and the wood grain. The length of the body and the shape of the f-holes. The slope of the bridge and the position of the sound-post. He told him about Eastern European and Chinese copies which were getting better and better and cost so little compared to new European ones. But, a truly hand-crafted instrument was still a joy to hold and he passed one of the violins to Billy to feel and look at the features.

It was smooth and cool as water and there was depth to the rich colours in the wood; Billy handled it as he would a new-born baby. The violin maker showed him the violin he was working on and one that he had repaired himself.

Eventually, he stopped.

"Forgive me for talking so much."

"No problem," said Billy.

"Do you have a violin you want repaired?"

"No."

"Do you want to buy one?"

"Not yet."

"You're just learning then?"

"I think I'd like to learn," he said, but his answer seemed so deeply inadequate. "How much are they?"

"They vary. Anywhere from less than a hundred pounds to several thousand. You can pay a million pounds if you want to, but not for one of mine." And he laughed gently.

"I was thinking more like £50 to £100," He looked away and turned back to the painting of the Po Valley.

The violin maker told him to come back in a week or so as he had some more violins coming in for repair and maybe he could sort something out for him. There was usually a way. He handed Billy a business card with his telephone number hand-written on it.

When Billy arrived at work on Monday morning he could hear Davey across the yard. When he got to the warehouse, the veins on Davey's neck were already tight and standing-out. He was toe to toe with the supervisor.

Both men were spluttering their rage at each other. The supervisor began prodding Davey in the shoulder telling him that he was just a pain-in-the-arse, bloody trouble-maker and his days in the company were fucking numbered. Him and all his fucking trouble-maker chums and he pointed at Billy. Davey swept the man's arm away, their wrists smacking into each other.

"This site is hanging on by its finger nails and you want to be some kind of working-class fucking hero."

"Button it, you Wee Twat," said Davey. He looked like he was going to have a heart attack.

A week later, Mrs Rae was dead. Billy was walking past her flat on the way from work and he saw a policewoman standing at her doorway. He asked what was the matter and she told him that her home help had found her dead in bed. Mrs Rae had been taken away for a post-mortem and she was standing there until the council came to board up her flat. They were looking to trace the immediate family and did he know of anyone?

The policewoman looked very young. Her bright eyes scanned Billy up and down. Her arms were crossed at the wrist in front of her stomach. Billy stared past her in to Mrs Rae's flat.

"She didn't have many friends," he said.

"Did you know her?"

"I shopped for her."

"You're not family then?"

"She used to call me *Son*."

There were only a few people at Mrs Rae's cremation a couple of weekends later. Being a Saturday, he thought that most of her friends and relatives could have made it. But there was just her daughter and her husband who had travelled from somewhere on the west coast. Other than these two and him, there were four other people, all old women from the estate. He nodded to them, but didn't talk. The minister was a woman and she spoke kindly of Mrs Rae but it was clear that she didn't know her.

There were no details to her life. The small things that marked her out. The fact that she watched nature programmes on the television and she listened to classical music on the radio while she made her small meals. During the hymns, no one sang, but taped music filled the silence.

Mrs Rae's daughter said a few words, then the minister said her final prayers and the coffin rolled forward for the curtains to part. Mrs Rae's daughter was sobbing uncontrollably. Her husband had his arm tightly around her shoulder. The older women were quite calm.

So this is how it all ends, thought Billy.

On the following Monday, for the first time in his life, he rang work to tell them he was ill. By half nine in the morning he was at the door of the violin maker. While Billy sat in his back room, the man made a cup of tea and offered him some biscuits. Billy said no, but the man brought some anyway. Afterwards he went through to the front room where he did all of the work on the violins and returned with a violin in a case with a bow. He brought a tutorial book, too.

"I can't teach you," he said "I'm afraid like most violin makers, I don't play. Not very well. We're all kind of dumb. I have a friend who teaches if you're interested. His name and phone number are at the top of that book. I borrowed it from him. He says you can keep it as long as you're playing the violin. If it suits, we'll work out a sort of rental on that one so you don't have to pay out too much money until you are sure you want to play. If you enjoy it we will talk about a price. Don't drop it," and he handed the case to him. "Have a go. Don't be shy. It's all tuned up." The man smiled.

He left to go into the front room, but said that Billy was welcome to stay a while and practice holding it and get the feel of it. When he was alone, Billy took the violin out of its case and looked at it. He ran his fingers across the strings and looked at it from various angles, the way the violin maker did when he first showed Billy the violins. Then, he took out the bow and tensioned it as he had been shown and, crooking the violin limply under his neck, he drew the bow across the strings. It gave a wavering, fragile, empty sound.

He shifted on his chair and sat with his back straight; he tightened the grip with his neck on the body of the violin. He tried to look serious. He imagined sunlight and a hundred violin makers; craftsmen slowly creating their delicate beauty.

He pulled the bow across the strings again; this time more confidently and with belief. The sound was much clearer.

"Very good," came a voice from the next room. "Much better. A pure note."

Stonewall

He never got a piece of stone wrong. Once he had it in his hand, he tossed it around, eyeing all the angles before he started at it with his walling hammer. After only a few strokes he would nestle it into the wall's face. The fragments went into the centre of the wall, and he began the search for the next stone. The bits in the centre of the wall he called the heart. He filled this up as the outer wall progressed.

"Keep your heart up, Helen," he said.

"Keep your heart up," I repeated, nodding.

And he sat down to eat the food I'd brought out for him. When he worked on the far fells, my mother brought the sandwiches to him otherwise she would not see him all day. When he was in the near fields, I took his food to him. He always told me dry-stone walling was man's work. In the rain, we crouched under any available trees. Otherwise, we took what meagre shelter the wall could give us. We sat with our backs to the wall that he had just built and he told me about the stone he was working and how easily it cut. Then, when he had eaten he stood up and set-to again without another word. Then I knew it was time to go. *Manswork*. Taking sandwiches must have been girl's work, which was why I did it.

He showed me the joints, the way different stone behaved, how to cut with the grain. Never put a stone down once he had it in his hand, but once he set-to, that was it. No more talk. Then, one Tuesday, taking me out of school, he drove us in the Landrover to the local town to get a new walling hammer. In the shop he stood at the counter and talked for a long time to the man who served. It was a conversation in some sort of code, with magical words that I did not understand, and a different rhythm, like the music of some foreign land.

So, I wandered off into the small shop. The shelves were piled high with things that I did not know the name or function of, and everywhere there was the smell of the paraffin heater, like sweet oil and animals. We had a paraffin heater in the barn for nights when the electricity went off and the young lambs needed to be kept warm. We had the heater on in the house at Christmas so the house was warm for Santa. Here, between rows of brushes and hammers and screws and tins of creosote, the smell from the heater followed me like a Christmas dream. Some of the tools had oil on them to stop them going rusty. I turned and looked in the deep caverns of the shop and passed the tins of creosote piled on shelves that were higher than my father. And there were vices and hammers heavier than I could lift and brushes on hooks so high that the man in the shop needed a stick or ladders to lift them down. As I walked past one row of saws hung on small hooks, I got too close and the fabric of my coat pulled against the teeth of one of the saws. A small tear was made in my coat, and the saw fell off its perch with a clatter.

And instantly my father was calling me from somewhere behind the rows and rows of shelves so I walked quickly through the maze to where he was standing, with his new hammer shining bright and starry in the shop lights and smelling of the paraffin, that sweet Christmas smell.

"You ready?" he asked.

We got into the Landrover in the dark that had now enveloped the street and the shop and the town around us. We travelled back in silence, his new hammer resting in my lap, its cold oily weight was as still as the stone he worked.

At home my father said;

"She was messing about. She ripped her coat."

Before I had time to reply he was off with the new hammer to put it into the tool shed, alongside the old one.

"I wasn't," I said and started to cry, but my mother told me the coat would soon mend and it wasn't my best one anyway. So we settled down to sew it before tea, whilst the sound of hammering and sawing came from beyond the closed kitchen door and across the yard.

"How did you meet dad?" I asked my mother as she sewed.

"We met at a dance."

"Did he talk to you?"

"Not much," she chortled.

And I saw them, in a different world dancing to a small band in a small hall, him with his hard, waller's hands and her with a fine cotton print dress. His hands would scratch and catch on the fabric of her clothes and he would treat her with the respect she deserved. Like a lady. That too is man's work.

At the county show in my repaired coat, I walked around with my mother whilst my father waited away from the main show-ground arena with his few friends waiting to enter the walling competition. In the main tent I went to see the exhibitions of photographs with themes like, "A winter's day."

and "Holidays." and cakes, "Fancy." and "Plain." and rows and rows of paper plates with five runner beans, or four eating apples or five tomatoes. There were rows of leeks, and potatoes and cauliflowers. Outside, the pens of sheep and cattle were emptied into the main arena from time to time, and the sheep dogs and handlers did their work. And all the while my father was building his small section of wall away from the main crowd; quietly, alone and never getting a piece of stone wrong. At the end of the day, he was announced the winner, as usual, and I clapped and jumped up and down as he collected the cup that would sit on our television for another year.

Sometime over the next winter, a scaffold went up around the church. My father pointed it out as we passed it in the Landrover. It rose up the tower and kept going. Then, with spring, men began to work on the stonework of the tower. This was too much for him to ignore, it seemed. As we drove by one clear weekend, he stopped.

We stood as he looked up the scaffolding that had risen. Eventually he shouted to the masons working above us.

"That's a grand day," he said.

"Aye."

"How's it going?"

"Fine."

Then, before I knew why he was talking to them, the two men had come down the ladders and were next to us. They spoke with the rhythm and the same mystery as the shop keeper. My father knew about stone and he told them that he did a lot of walling around here, out on the fells. They seemed fascinated by what he had to say and listened silently as he spoke, making me proud of my father. He told them of the quarry that produced the stone for the church, how it was grained and how it varied across the quarry face.

"They knew about stone, back then," my father said.

"Aye," said one of the builders.

"Can she have a look?" he asked, pointing to me.

"Don't see why not."

"Come on then, Young 'un," said the other man.

I followed the man, along with my father, up the levels of scaffolding, going from one platform to the next, zigzagging our way up the metal structure. I was scared of heights, but did not want to let my father down so I kept on going. We rose up the outside of the church tower until we stood, tightly packed on the platform next to the highest part of the church. Scattered around lay the men's tools and small pieces of stone where they had been taking out blocks to replace them. I walked on my own round the tower to look out over the village and beyond to the distant fells. I held tight onto the scaffold rail. I felt the wind off the hills hitting my face. Behind me, with my hand outstretched, I could feel the cold stone of the church tower. I could see our farm. Then one of the builders came round to see me, and left my father talking to his colleague. He pointed out the variations in the stone, and he ran his rough hands down it as he spoke. I could hear his hand make a noise like my father when he sandpapered wood in his shed. Then the man pointed to the carved pieces of stone, small details lost in the weathering. He told me to look at the love that had gone into making the individual blocks and carvings; he used the word love over and over. The people who did this never thought that anyone would ever see it this close again, he told me, yet they still put their whole soul into it.

"You're a lucky girl to see this," he said.

The man returned to his friend, and I stood on the platform alone with my fear of heights, and the wind around me and the love of the stonemasons at my back. Keep your heart up, I thought. I ran my hand down the stones of the tower but they did not make the sandpaper sound like the man's did. I edged forward to look directly down the tower and the scaffolding to where our Landrover was parked. I held onto the cold metal of the scaffold-pole and stared at the ground. Then my father called me and I was descending again. Walking to the Landrover, I showed my father a piece of stone that the man had given me, and I told him I was going to keep it forever.

"Do you love your job?" I asked him.

"What a daft question."

"Do you?"

"I enjoy it," he said.

"Do you love it?"

"Enough questions," he laughed.

So I left him and skipped back to the car. Next time we passed the church he pointed to the tower and said.

"You've been up there."

He said it every time we passed the church, and it became a ritual even after the scaffolding had disappeared. He said it to whoever was in the car. The only elaboration he made was to tell some people, particularly my friends, that "She was scared stiff." He said it when we drove past it on the way to school, and after he had picked me up from the bus stop when I returned from the local college and then from University; "You've been up there. You were scared stiff," he would say. And when I started to drive myself back on visits after I left home, I still thought to myself "I've been up there. I was scared stiff."

And so, as I drive past the church now, heading into the town at Christmas, with the jingle-bells excitement in my head, I am thinking "I've been up there. And I was scared stiff." In my parents' house, I light up the paraffin heater to get the sweet smell off it. I take my mother into town to help with the Christmas shopping. We talk of my house, my work, of my friends, I talk to her about the farm. When we meet people in town that she knows, she says to them, "You remember Helen. She's an architect now."

Over coffee in the new café she says, "Your dad hates it in here."

"Why?"

"He hates the frothy coffee."

"How is he?"

"Not good. Bored mostly now he's had to give up walling. He's mellowed, though."

He's now at home most of the time, tripping her up around the house, she says. My mother suggests that I should take my father to the new office I've built at the back of my house. "He'll be so proud."

After Christmas, I take him in the car over the open fells, down the motorway and through the suburbs of the town and into the small knot of older houses and buildings where my house is. I try to explain that it's like a village set in the heart of the city, but I don't think he's convinced. Inside, I offer him tea, but he doesn't want it. I suggest we go down the road to the café to get a frothy coffee and he smiles.

"Has your mother been talking?"

I show him round the house. He spends his time running his hands, still large and rough despite doing no work with them now, along the internal walls and looking at the doors and woodwork. He says he likes the quality of the doors, and I tell him they are original. I realise I am waiting for his approval, but none is forthcoming. In my rush to fill the silence, I tell him that the plaster-work is also 19th Century, and that I intend to take the floorboards and the other fittings back to the original Victorian.

"Back to the original, eh?" he repeats, nodding.

My office is in a converted shed at the rear of the house. To get there, we need to go out of the backdoor. Outside he again runs his hand along the stonework.

"Good stone. Pointing needs a bit of work," he says, and in the office he looks around at the computers. He wanders up and down my desks and display screens. I explain that one is for emails and written work and that the other, the Apple, is for design and visual work. I switch it on, and wait for it to bring up an image. Then I hunt around in the photographic library and eventually come up with a picture of the village church back home. My father turns round from having been looking at some of the plans on the drawing board, and moves over to the machine. He watches in silence as I flick through the various images I have of the church. First its exterior, and then its interior. I tell him that I've just received a commission for a piece of work to extend a church in the city; one that was worked on by the same architect who also worked on the restoration of our church many years ago.

"Scott?" he asks.

"Yes."

"George Gilbert Scott. He got everywhere."

I reproach myself for being surprised my father knows about the architect. He asks to see my plans, but I have to tell him I have not started work on them yet.

I won the commission when my name was put forward by a member of the congregation after I had worked on their house. My research followed the trail of George Gilbert Scott around the country. Endless websites told me of his restoration work to more churches and cathedrals than can be remembered. Of course, there were also his big commissions in London. The confidence of him and the volume of his work daunted me. House extensions were one thing, but this was different. *Manswork* I'd thought. Did I love my work enough and did I love the church enough to change it? Or to follow on from George Gilbert Scott. I read more and more about him, convincing myself I needed a better feel for his work. I looked at his buildings on photo-libraries across many websites. I looked at the details, the cut of the stone, his recurring techniques, the context. I looked at it all. I spent a long time looking at the images of the church in my parents' village: the exterior, the additions, the restoration work. I found *A view from the tower*, and there was the village, the fells and snaking up the hill, the dark line of one of my father's stone walls.

I've been up there. I was scared stiff.

On one occasion, when he was working on a wall out on the fells - perhaps even the wall on the image - I took my father his lunch. We huddled in the rain behind the section he had just finished. It was a Sunday, and my mother was at home in the kitchen. He had been on with this length of wall for nearly a week. When we'd finished eating, instead of setting-to straight away, he asked me what I wanted to be when I grew up. I told him I did not know.

He picked up his new walling hammer and he gave it to

me.

"Let's see how you do at this," he said, and he asked me to find a piece of stone to fit into the wall. I picked one up and offered it to him. He told me that wouldn't do and dropped it, picking up a different one and passing it to me. I tapped ineffectually at it a few times, until he pointed to a particular point and told me:

"Whack it there." I hit it, and the stone split along an invisible plane and fit neatly into the next gap in the wall. I put the smaller piece into the centre of the wall. Keep your heart up I thought. I went through the process a few more times but eventually handed the hammer back.

"I can't do it with someone watching over my shoulder," I said.

"You can do anything you want if you set your mind to it."

As I left, he passed me a small piece of stone that I had broken off one of the larger pieces. I put it in my pocket.

In my office, at the computer, I continue to show my father the images of our church. After he has looked at them, he moves around the office. He stands next to the drawing board, where he picks up the two pieces of stone lying on its upper edge.

"One is a heart and the other is love." I say.

"I'll take your word for it."

He puts them down and asks me why I haven't any drawings to show him. I explain about my research and how I need to have a good understanding of the grain of the man's work. As a distraction I pull out some photographs for the commission that I have not yet loaded onto the machine. It is a church that has grown up through the centuries with differing types of stone; different jointing and detail. But mostly, it has been worked on by Scott and it has his feel to it. My extension will abut directly onto his last addition. In one of the photographs, there is scaffolding which was put up to allow me to look at some of his work at close quarters.

"Have you been up there?" asks my father.

"Several times."

"And were you scared stiff?"

"A little," I say.

"And are you still scared?"

He doesn't wait for an answer but says he must leave me because he needs to let me work. I sit at my drawing board, which is linked to the computer screen electronically. Holding my electronic pen, I stare at the blank screen away to my right. I am still staring at it when my father returns from the house holding two mugs of tea and some sandwiches. He sits down next to me and glances at the blank screen. We eat in silence. When we have finished, he rises and picks up my plate and mug.

"You'll be wanting to set to," he says.

As he is going, he nods in the direction of the screen, because his two hands are full.

"There's no one looking over your shoulder now," he says.

I watch him leave my office and walk across the small yard. Through the window of my house I see him go into the living-room and nestle in one of my armchairs, where he sits and stares into the emptiness.

I turn from watching him to look at the blank screen and pick up my drawing pen again, but this time I move it across the page.

Tentatively at first, I begin to rough out the shape of the church and its orientation and where my extension will go. On the computer, the walls and outline of the church take shape. My pen brings up images of what is there and the walls I will build; dark lines growing against the brightness of the screen. Once the broad shape is in place, I look up and through the window of my office I see my father still sitting in the half-light of the living-room, staring, his eyes half closed. I look back at the screen and set to once more.

I will complete some more of the sketches before I go to call him and show him the walls that I have built.

Diving In

He liked to arrive early at the swimming pool when only a few people were there. Or, better still, like today, he loved being first when it was empty and the bright water billowed gently like a cloth-of-light underneath the skylights above his head.

He curled his feet round the cool tiles on the pool-side; he felt their smoothness fit comfortingly under his toes before he breathed deeply and dived into the empty pool. He stayed under the water for as long as he could, but with the years since his retirement he couldn't hold his breath very well. When he surfaced half-way along the pool he had to take a few deep gulps of the antiseptic air and then, as usual, swam ten lengths without stopping.

After his set of lengths, he rested and watched as a young woman and her daughter came into the pool. The woman carefully dropped into the water and stood waiting for the turbulence to subside before gently coaxing her small daughter to slide in. When the girl was in the water, he set off again for his next ten lengths, moving away from the woman to allow her more room.

The pool never got busy. From the outside, its old Victorian exterior was off-putting and austere. The front steps made access difficult while inside the wrought iron roof supports, which may once have been beautiful and confident, were beginning to rust. The old changing cubicles around the pool's edge could still be used, but most people preferred to get changed in the temporary buildings stuck onto the back of the main hall. The building was like a decaying seaside town that had known greatness, but was now aware of its own mortality. It just needed a bit of tender loving care, he thought, but then maybe it was already too late. Old things cannot always be changed.

When he had finished his second set of lengths he again stood up with his back to the pool-side and watched the woman and her child. The three of them still had the pool to themselves. He recognised most of the people who came into the baths in the mornings; retired people and young mothers mostly, but he did not know her. It was possibly because she was so calm and quiet that he had not noticed her before. She had gently slipped into the pool and unassumingly got on with teaching her child.

On his way out of the baths he saw the small hand-written note on the window of the pay-booth. It stated very simply that the baths would be closing at the end of summer for refurbishment. The note had appeared without any warning several weeks ago and since then he had spent much of the time thinking where else he could go to swim; he had no idea where the next nearest swimming pool was. Besides, it was bound to be busy and have slides and god-forbid a wave machine. He didn't like change anymore; he wasn't good at it, not since his wife died. He hadn't noticed how difficult it was making decisions without her until she was gone. But she would have known what to do, or at least convince him that he knew already; yet without her he had fretted ever since the notice went up. He should probably speak to one of the other pool users.

The next morning he left early to go to the baths; there was no-one on duty when he got there so he just walked straight in. The staff had almost given up already. He was first there so after he had dived in, he tried to swim a length under water. He once more fell short, but carried on into his usual ten lengths and got into his rhythm. He loved the routine; the predictability of it. He alternated one length free-style and one length breast-stroke then stopped after ten lengths.

As he swam, a few other people came in. The men dived in with a lot of noise and splashing and, like him, set off on a set of lengths. The women dropped smoothly into the water and set off very quietly. And the quietest of them all was the young mother and her daughter. As he finished his tenth length, he saw her slip into the water and, having waited for the young girl to steady herself, coax her into the pool.

After the girl slid in, the woman lifted her out onto the pool side and stood her on the edge and got her to put her arms down by her side. Then her mother gently helped her to jump into the pool and after he had watched the girl make this first hesitant leap from the pool side, he set off to do more lengths.

As he was leaving the building after getting changed, he saw the woman with her daughter standing on the steps outside. He still hadn't talked to anyone about the sign so he approached her.

"The pool is closing," he said.

"I saw the sign, yes."

"Where will you go?"

"We'll find somewhere. There's always something else."

"Perhaps we could start a petition."

"I'm sure it won't help."

"Your little girl is coming on well, though."

"We'll get there in the end, won't we poppet," she said looking down at the girl. The woman said that they needed to catch a bus, and turned to walk off along the street holding her daughter's hand. The girl looked round to wave good -bye to him, then trotted alongside her mother, happy in the sunshine.

Over the next weeks, fewer and fewer people came to the pool in the mornings and it grew more depressing inside. The cubicles, once brightly painted in blue with red and white striped canvas curtains, were taped off so no-one could use them. On one morning, one of the tiles came off as he dived in, but he did not report it in case they simply shut the pool. But still, on most days, when he was part way through his first ten lengths, the woman arrived with the girl and with each day he watched the girl practice tumbling in and he watched too the patience of the woman. It became clear she was teaching her daughter how to dive. The first part had been to get her to jump in, now she was getting her to tip into the water from a sitting position. Next she would get her to crouch and finally stand.

He began to look forward to this almost as much as his swim. In some ways, he looked forward to it more. After all, unlike him, she was progressing, wasn't she? He'd seen her start with that first noisy flop into the water and here she was, kneeling on one knee, pointing her arms into the air.... that's it, poppet, that's it, point them all the way up to the ceiling, as if you are trying to push through the high windows into the blue sky.... pointing her arms into the air and pushing off into a brief arc before she sank beneath the water to come up spluttering and smiling with her small leap into something new.

"She's getting there," he said to the woman on the way out.

"She's doing brilliantly."

"What's her name?"

"Sarita."

"You can nearly dive, Sarita," he said crouching down to her level.

"I can nearly do lots of things."

He didn't see them for a couple of days and the next time they appeared he had already finished his first set of lengths and was sitting on the pool side when they arrived. The woman smiled briefly at him, then got on with her teaching. He remained sitting on the pool side watching the delicate choreography between the mother and the child. As Sarita bent down on one knee, preparing to dive, her mother moved forward in the water to give her confidence then, when the girl looked settled, she moved slightly backwards to give her more space; a slight nod of the head told Sarita when it was time to make the kneeling dive. As she hit the water, her mother again stepped forward and held out her arm to act as a support, but only just long enough to make sure she went off again on her own.

"See if you can swim a width for me," she said, and Sarita set off across the pool while her mother watched her.

The woman's movements could easily have been missed, but they were signs of deep understanding. This is what he missed most from his wife; the silences and small gestures that could have been misunderstood or taken for indifference.

Watching Sarita's mother, he remembered when his own daughter had got married and the car had pulled away after the reception taking her on the honeymoon. He had played the happy fool all day; at least that's one off my hands, he'd said, someone else can worry about her now, don't mind if I do.... a small malt whisky would be lovely. Great swathes of smoke hung around him from the cigarettes and there was much hand shaking and arm slapping. But when the car moved off with his daughter, the realisation she had left swept over him like an ocean yet, without noticing her arrival, his wife was there by his side, linking her arm into his.

"I'm cold," she said, so he took his jacket off and put it round her shoulders. "Give me a hug," she added, knowing he needed one as much as she did. And back inside the hotel reception, she was right when she took a full glass of whisky off him because he'd probably had enough. Just as she was right a week later when she suggested he stop smoking; so he stopped after thirty years.

When Sarita finished her width, her mother lifted her up and put her on the side of the pool again so that she could try another kneeling dive. He set off on his next set of ten lengths, the cool water clearing his head. As he swam, he saw out of the corner of his eye Sarita repeatedly crouching on one knee and diving in. At the end of his second set of lengths he went over to the couple.

"Have you decided where you are going to go when this place shuts?" he asked the woman.

"Not yet...and you?"

"No idea."

"It's fine just now, though. Nice and quiet to practice our

diving. You've got to take the opportunity, haven't you?"

He looked down at Sarita and asked her how she was today. She pointed to a plaster on her knee.

"I cut myself, but the man put a plaster on me." The woman explained that one of the tiles in the changing room had come off and the sharp edge had cut her while she got ready.

"I'm going to dive properly next week," Sarita added.

"Then you can teach *me* to dive-in," he said.

"I like your goggles," she said.

He smiled and left them to get on with their swimming while he returned to his routine. His wife had bought him the goggles, just as it was her who had first coaxed him into swimming. She had suggested that he exercise as he approached his retirement and then, each week, she asked him how far he had got with his swimming. Without asking, she had gently urged him to progress. The first time he came back and said that he had done ten lengths without stopping, she took him out for lunch to celebrate. When he did twenty lengths, she bought him a pair of swimming goggles with black lenses.

"I can't wear those," he had said.

"Of course you can. They'll make you look professional."

"I'll look stupid."

"You'll look sexy."

Their own delicate choreography, he thought as he wrapped his trunks and the goggles into his damp towel and left the pool alone.

The following week, he arrived first nearly every day so as not to miss Sarita and her mother, but they did not turn up. On the Thursday, he dived in and held his breath as he swam and struggled, but after all these months of trying he managed to reach the other end. As he touched the wall, he came up spluttering and gasping, but he had finally swum a length under water. He wondered what kind of a fuss his wife would have made over that.

As he got his breath back, Sarita and her mother came in; there was no-one else in the pool. He kept an eye on them as he swam and when Sarita finally stood on the pool side preparing to dive properly for the first time, he stopped his swimming and stood in the shallow end, watching.

Sarita's mother whispered something to the girl then withdrew to the centre of the pool. The girl raised her arms; she was on her own now. She shuffled uneasily on the tiles, then lowered her arms. Her mother smiled at her and pointed to the ceiling and Sarita raised her arms again. And this was it, he thought. Sarita bent her legs slightly and, after a vague nod from her mother, pushed herself off into a high arc. He saw a few drops of water fall from her body as she curved into the brightness of the skylights before disappearing into the water. When she came up, her mother was already at her side, kissing and hugging her and he too started to clap and shout, well done, Sarita, well done. By the time he had finished his last length, she was confidently diving in, again and again.

He waited for them outside in the sunshine. When they emerged, he went straight to Sarita. He took out his goggles with the black lenses and, bending down to her level, handed them to her.

"These are for you. To say well done for learning to dive-in."

The girl took them saying thank-you three or four times. As he rose, her mother said, "That is such a nice thing to do.

Thank you."

As she spoke, she put out her hand and held lightly onto his bare arm. It was a gesture which, he thought later, she must do all the time, but its intimacy awakened him. He felt the smooth skin of her fingers softly raising the hairs on the back of his hand; her thumb rested faintly under his wrist near his pulse point. He looked at the woman's face properly; he had not looked at anyone's face in such detail for a long time. He was conscious of her wet hair dripping onto her bare shoulders, the small trails of water running down to the straps of her deep red dress; he saw small dark patches beginning to appear in the material where the water was soaking through. He looked down to make sure her hand was still there; the touch of it on his arm was so light it was almost imperceptible. He felt a slight breeze pass them in the sunshine and he saw that it raised goose-bumps on her skin. Her touch relaxed even more; a hand was hovering ghost-like above his own skin. What it was to have forgotten such gentleness, such closeness.

He looked up at the woman's smiling face again.

"It was nothing," he said,

She removed her hand, took hold of Sarita's and said good-bye. They turned away and Sarita skipped alongside her mother, twirling the goggles on her finger as she walked. When they reached the corner of the street they both turned and waved to him and he returned the wave before they went out of sight.

Over the weekend, he did not go swimming, but he felt a new enthusiasm for organising his life. He made a list of new pools that he might go to when the old one closed. He thought about taking it to show Sarita and her mother, so they could start at the new pool together. He also cleaned his small house, taking care to polish the photographs of his wife. On Sunday, he rang his daughter.

On the Monday morning he got up early and, instead of putting on his usual old clothes, he wore some of his newer ones. He even put on a jacket, something he hadn't done for many months, but today it felt right as he was even thinking of asking Sarita and her mother if they fancied a cup of tea in the café opposite after their swim. He looked out of his window before leaving; it was raining and a breeze blew the rain in sheets along the street. Nonetheless, he set-off early for the pool, thinking that he might try forty lengths today.

But as he got off the bus and looked along the street, he saw a group of people standing in front of the baths. When he got nearer he saw that they were Council officials putting up a notice to say that the pool was closed. One was running yellow and red tape through the bright brass door-handles and round the stone pillars at the top of the steps.

"The roof's leaking," said one of the men. "It's got to close now."

When they had put up their signs and tied off the tape, they went, leaving him alone on the pavement staring at the building. He stood for half an hour under the eaves, then waited in the café across the road, but when work-men arrived to board-up the pool, he knew he finally had to move on. He set off, now feeling ridiculous in his new jacket. By the time he got on the bus Sarita and her mother had still not appeared and he knew they were not going to come.

After that, he passed the boarded–up pool each time he went into town on the bus. He watched as the fly posters for DJs and concerts began to appear on the walls, and then began to fade after the summer. The windows got smashed and the boarding was pulled away by people trying to get in; rubbish and fly-tipping accumulated in deepening drifts around the site. In preparation for the building's demolition, a metal fence arose around it so the site looked like a military base. When the bulldozers moved in, the site was cleared until only the void of the pool was left, partly filled with rubble and the timber from the fallen cubicles. Then, each time he passed, the rubble slowly disappeared until finally the site was cleared and the building only existed in his imagination, like the memory of his wife, the ghostly touch on his skin and the image of Sarita diving, somewhere, into bright new waters.

Wish You Well

Much of what you read here you will recognise as true.

There is a sign on the Georgian buildings along Palace Road in Dublin which reads "Sick and Indigent Roomkeepers' Society: Founded 1790." You said that you loved the sound of those words.

And down the road from there, on Cork Hill, there's that café which serves great coffee and huge cakes. And it was there we sat and talked after our first run, months before we had sex. You bought the cakes; it was your treat you said.

"Grab it while you can," you said.

"Is that what you think?"

"You'll learn."

When we left, we went back to your house in the north of the Liberties on Hanover Lane; you said that it was ironic that an English woman lived somewhere called Hanover Lane. Imperialism works at the architectural level, too, you said. You knew things like that.

We'd met not long before, in The Winding Stair bookshop on Ormond Quay next to the river. This much you know. It was in the room at the top where you were to recite some of your work, but I was just looking for any-old-thing to read. I saw you sitting, thin-limbed and tanned; bare-legged in a summer dress, as you looked round the room over your finely-perched glasses. I would never have guessed your age.

A man I assumed was the owner introduced you as a well-known writer from across the water. There were copies of your new book of poems in a crisp neat pile on the desk at the front. The tiny room was full and it was difficult to squeeze out past the people, so I stayed to listen. I didn't read poetry usually. But none of this was usual.

You stood and held the book in your left hand. Your right hand swooped and then hovered like a hawk as you spoke. Between your poems you joked and people laughed at things I did not understand. Afterwards, I queued to buy a copy and to get your signature, but mostly I wanted to see up-close the lithe animated woman you had become.

"I like your poems," I said as you signed.

"Thank you. You're English?"

"Doing a Masters at Trinity."

"Do you fancy coming for a drink? There's a few of us going."

I was still carrying the book when I met up with you and your friends at O'Donohughe's that night. The back bar was full of foreign tourists looking for traditional music, so we stayed in the front where the crowd pushed us closer and closer together until I could smell the scent of you, see the small creases around your mouth, the gently ageing skin on your hands, but also the azure of your eyes. I could not have said when I became aware you were flirting. Looking back, maybe it was when you first put your hand on my arm and asked what I did to keep fit.

"I run."

"A healthy mind in a healthy body."

"Not much of either."

"We'll see."

You briefly left your hand on my wrist and, when the man from the Winding Stair brought back another round of stout without spilling a drop, he said to me, in a way I took to be a joke: "Careful with that one, laddo. She'll suck you in and blow you out in tiny bubbles."

You smiled and lowered your eyes.

After the bar closed, we walked home; you, me and the man from the Winding Stair. I took comfort in the familiarity of strangers. We left you at the door to your house on Hanover Street, then he came with me to make sure I found my way home too. On the way, he explained that he was not the owner of the book shop, or the manager. Good God, no. If only. No. He was just a humble lecturer at Trinity and you were his latest secret weapon. Their visiting writer-in-residence for the next year. You were to help teach the n'ere-do-wells and miscreants how to write poetry and novels and all manner of wondrous things. You were to give lectures to the great unwashed and lead some seminars for the non-believers. However, be that as it may, and here was the rub, you came with a reputation as a bit of a wild woman; hell, you'd written poems on that very subject. That's why they'd appointed you. Shake things up a bit. Mind you, women generally got like that when they reached... you know... a certain age. That's something I'd learn in my own time. Any way, he thought you were a fierce and fabulous woman. A bit like the mighty Maeve. Only thinner, or so he imagined, as he had never actually seen Maeve. But I wasn't to pay too much attention to him anyway as he was happily married and more than a bit drunk.

I turned up at your house a few days later. In O'Donohughe's you'd asked me to teach you to run. I said that no-one needed teaching, but you enthused that you'd always wanted a personal trainer. In exchange, you would help me start writing, although you said no-one needed teaching to do that, either. I'd never thought about writing, but said I'd go for a few runs anyway. When I arrived, you met me at the door and showed me in.

The kitchen was full and you introduced me to your housemates. Three men: Toner, Peewee and Clarkey. And Sarah, a student from County Wicklow and the only one, it seemed, who had a proper name. The men were sitting round a table playing cards, cans of beer in front of them. Sarah was sitting in a battered armchair next to the stove.

"And you are?" asked Toner.

"Robin," I said.

"And I'm fucking Batman."

Peewee snorted and sprayed some beer on his cards. He wiped them on his sleeve.

"Jesus, you messy fucker."

"It's his fault."

"What kind of a name is Robin?

"We can't call him that. It's too English."

So from then on I was called Toyboy and was made instantly more welcome by them than I had ever been by anyone I can remember.

Our first run that early evening took us along the canal and on to Ball's Bridge; just to see what a Ball's Bridge looked like, you said. Afterwards, having sat through an hour of Toner and Peewee taking the piss out of you in your track suit, we went to that café on Cork Hill and from then-on that's where you took me after every run.

To start with I bored the arse off you (your phrase) with talk about training and heart rates, but eventually we got on to you and your writing and what I wanted to do when I grew-up (my phrase). Until then I had lived my life by easy codes and at first I was unused to your intensity. Your experience, the things you knew, your pursuit of what you called the truth. What had I ever cared what people thought was the truth? How did I know what I would end up doing with my life? Men have simpler needs; a straightforward view of things.

"You'll learn," you said. "If not, I'll teach you."

You succeeded in convincing me that I should come to one of your writing workshops.

When I turned-up some time later, I stood at the back of your evening-class, not wanting to venture in without being asked. You looked up and saw me and beckoned with your hand the one with the big amber ring - almost without skipping a beat as you read through the poetry. I took up my place at your bidding on the edge of your small intense semi-circle of people. You finished your reading to the group and led the discussion before getting one of them to read out their work. You picked over it forensically; there was one word that you made us search for, as you were unhappy with what was written. I can't remember now. Was it *love*, or *affection* or something else? Eventually, the meaning almost disappeared, but you seemed to enjoy the hunt.

After the workshop, you announced that we should all go to O'Donohughe's. You introduced me as your personal trainer and took my arm as we left the room in what I assumed was a motherly way, but was beginning to hope was something else.

O'Donohughe's was filling up, but we found a table in the backroom. I went to buy a round and by the time I got back you were already holding court in your small group. I sat on a low stool with my back to the room and watched you and the class talking about your work. I was unaware that behind me people were arriving with instruments, setting up for the night's session. It was only when the *Rakes of Kildare* started up that I knew about it. As I turned round to watch, you and your students pulled out the notebooks that you had said they must always carry and began to scribble as the music pulsed. At the end of the first set of tunes, you were still writing and you seemed to have missed all the music.

As the tunes flowed, you worked the people around you. The men melted at your attention; the women loved your intimacy. You were becoming, as ever, everyone's new best friend and I marvelled at your ability to do that. As the music swelled and throbbed, you flirted outrageously, as only a confident person can. You made notes, too, that the others strained to see as you jotted them down.

When we all left, you took someone else's arm as we turned off down Merrion Row. The door opened and closed behind us, the music came then went on the evening air.

You walked on ahead, the rest of us following behind talking quietly, aware that we couldn't compete with the energy you created with your laughing and occasional scream. It was after one rough, sexy laugh that a group of men whistled at you across the road, and you shouted something back. Then at the corner of St Stephen's Green, you turned off, still with the man on your arm and I went off quietly to my flat.

The next day, I came to your house for our usual run, but you were not up.

"Heavy night," said Toner.

They were all in the kitchen as usual, with Sarah sitting next to the cooker with the gas ring turned on to keep warm and the rest of them sitting round the table, cards already out. Toner dealt the cards, dealing me in.

"Come on. We'll take your money off you while she gets up."

"Lambs to the slaughter, Peewee," said Clarkey, "Lambs to the slaughter."

"Nine card brag."

"Three's high."

"Just get on with it."

"Careful Toyboy, you're surrounded by shysters."

"Just play the cards, will you."

"That's all we can ever do, just play the cards we're dealt."

"Philosophical, Peewee?" asked Sarah.

"Sarah, it's the burden of my life."

By the time you came down I'd almost learned to play nine-card brag, but I was thirty Euros down. Sarah had pulled her chair up from next to the cooker and was helping me play my hands and make the best of the cards I'd been dealt. Just before we set off for our run Toner pushed the money back towards me.

"Take it back. It was too easy, Toyboy."

"You can buy us all a pint sometime," said Clarkey.

"It'll be a pleasure to drink your money."

I left Sarah ten Euros to play-on with.

Our weeks slipped past with the rhythm of runs and nine

card brag and nights in the backroom of O'Donohughe's. I continued coming to some of your evening classes and watched the poems and tales from nights-full-of-sessions take shape.

We ran and drank and played cards and sat and talked.

I never thought much about any of it. I never analysed the happiness; it was only when the sadness came that I started to think.

I got the chance to buy the drinks I owed when we met up in the winter warmth of the backroom of O'Donohughe's one Friday. It was Clarkey's birthday and they'd been there all day, but you and I and Sarah caught up with them later. They were drunk already and the cards were out with heaps of money on the table, but Peewee cleared it all away when we arrived.

I sat between you and Sarah, who started to ask me about my course; we didn't get much chance to talk in the house, she said. Always too noisy, but they were a good bunch. And had I ever been to County Wicklow; perhaps I might like to go. The Wicklow Mountains were famous. It was very beautiful. I really ought to go, you know. She could show me round; she'd enjoy that.

I turned to you at a break in our conversation and you were looking around the room with that serenity that comes with age. A kind of aloofness that makes men think that they can fall in love with you, but probably also means that they shouldn't.

I guess that you know you can look like that. We live in a self-conscious age and you know these things better than most.

"Who wants a drink?" I asked as I got up to go to the bar, but Clarkey pulled me back down again.

"But it's my shout," I said.

"What does it matter whose round it is?"

"Let Toyboy buy us a drink."

"Listen, we're only here once on this miserable earth. It's my birthday, so I'll decide whose buying the feckin' drinks." And he stood up and instantly fell over Sarah's stool. As he stumbled, he pushed me back on to your knees. We laughed at his fall and the mess he made of standing up again, but when I looked at you, you were staring at me as I nestled into your lap.

That probably clinched it.

We left the pub together with a few hangers-on including the man from the Winding Stair. We were a loud, tight clump of people bouncing their way from wall to wall through the night-time Dublin streets. Once we got back to your kitchen, the booze and the cards and the fags came out and everyone sat round talking and drinking and playing nine card brag and five card stud and anything else people called out.

"Lambs to the slaughter," shouted Toner as we drank.

I'm not sure how we finally ended up together. I know we were drunk, so when you suggested staying the night - it was after all a long way home - I just agreed and you said you'd find me a bed and then there we were, naked together, your slender limbs wrapping round me like ivy, the smell of drink on your breath and you asking to keep the lights off.

When I woke in the morning you were already getting dressed; you said you had a seminar to attend. You walked across the dimly lit room in your bra and knickers. You brushed your hair, leaning over, attacking it in long strokes. You put on your clothes and came over to get some perfume from the bedside cabinet. I leaned across and put my hand on your thigh and began to run it up your leg, not sure if that's what I should do. You moved my hand and said, "I'll be late. I'll give you a call."

Before you left, you looked again at yourself in the mirror then you rubbed down the front of your dress with your hands. Turning sideways to look at your profile you asked, almost to yourself, whether you looked fat in that skirt. You patted your stomach. It was the first and only time I'd seen you unsure of anything.

Then you were gone.

I went downstairs, knowing I was not coming down to the same kitchen and would never do so again. Toner, Peewee and Clarkey were already there with their hangovers. The chair by the cooker was empty.

"Lambs to the slaughter," said Peewee.

"Give him a break."

"Where's Sarah?" I asked.

"Said she had to go home."

"All of a sudden," said Toner. "To the beautiful County Wicklow."

You rang me later and said that you couldn't make that evening's run; in fact you'd been thinking about it and probably wanted to give it all a rest for a while.

From then on, it proved difficult to see you, so I came to one of your workshops. Your class was reading-out their poems, some from that first night in O'Donohughes. There was a collection of the poems coming out as a pamphlet and you wanted to get them right. I stood well to the back this time, beyond the darkness that encroached. As you analysed the poems in the spotlight from one of the overhead lights, I briefly envied once more the certainty that glowed around you.

The way you searched for the right words, seeking to pluck them from the air as if that would lead you to the truth.

We went for our last coffee on Cork Hill.

"I'm sorry," you said, getting up to leave when we'd finished our drinks.

"There's nothing to be sorry about."

"I need to sort myself out."

You left, giving me a small kiss on my cheek. I felt the wet patch with my fingers then I stopped when I became aware of an elderly couple watching me. As I caught the eye of the man, he smiled at me.

You told me often enough that writing helps get to the heart of things, somewhere near the truth, so I wrote this to help me understand. You see, to tell you the truth, I did believe that there was something there, if only for an instant. Something like friendship, attraction; certainly not love, but affection maybe. You tell me the word. You're good with words.

When it was time for me to leave Dublin I hadn't seen you for months. I rang you to leave a message...to wish you well...but I got no reply.

I was taken to the ferry by Toner, Peewee, Clarkey and the man from the Winding Stair who had adopted them as his friends. He sat next to me in the back of the car.

He told me that he'd heard I'd gone a bit astray in his dark and dangerous city. But these things happened, he supposed. God, even his own marriage went astray from time to time. Besides, hadn't he warned me you were a wild one? And I should have listened to him because, contrary to popular belief and despite what he said the first time, when he had actually been only a bit married but very happily drunk...anyway, where was he? Hadn't he told me the last time that you would suck me in and blow me out in tiny bubbles? Isn't that what he'd said? And hadn't that materialised? However, and here was the Rub, with a capital "R", you were doing the business with the students. You were a damned good teacher, a damned good poet and they loved you. Still, I was only young and we all had to learn the hard way.

"What say you, Toner?" said the man from the Winding Stair.

"I'd say you need to give it a rest."

"She's as mixed up as the rest of us," I said.

"Mixed up, my arse," said the man from the Winding Stair. "She knows just what she's doing."

"I said I think you should give it a rest," repeated Toner.

"Consider it done." And he let the subject drop with a couple of comments to the effect that there are plenty more fish in the sea, but, in a different life, he wouldn't have minded a crack at the mighty Maeve himself given half a chance and a fair wind, present company excepted.

When we got to the ferry terminal they waited with me until it was time to sail. Just before I boarded, Toner handed me a piece of paper and I put it in my pocket.

From the boat, I watched them wave and return to the car for a night on the town. The light was fading fast as they pulled away. Up on deck, I opened the piece of paper. It was Sarah's phone number, written in Toner's spidery handwriting, in which he'd written-out dozens of I.O.U.s for me - I'd got much better at nine-card brag.

As we set sail into the spreading dusk, over the lough I could still make out the silhouette of the Wicklow Mountains in the pale distance. A string of house-lights close to the water's edge animated the foreground.

Perhaps I might get to the Wicklow Mountains one day, but right then I doubted it. It was already too full of echoes.

I folded the paper and put it into my wallet.

When it got too dark to see, I went down to the bar and ordered a pint and, toasting the people in your house, took out a notebook and started on this.

So here it is.

This is my truth; and I'm sure you will tell me yours one day.

And possibly read it out in a workshop somewhere in front of wide-eyed strangers who are set to become your new best-friends. Who knows, some of them may even believe they are already in love with you.

Acknowledgements

Several of these stories first appeared in other journals and literary publications, including Stand, Iron, Staple, Route and Chapman. A couple won competitions, including the Biscuit Publishing International Prize. Thanks to all those involved with these and other dedicated publishing and literary ventures and to the smaller and independent bookshops who support them. Thanks too for all those who have read and commented on my work, particularly my family and friends. Thanks are also due to my colleagues at Silver Quill, particularly Iona, Oliver and Wendy. And, as ever, thanks to Chris for his professionalism and enthusiasm in all matters about books and design.

For more information, please visit www.petebromwrites.co.uk